CLEANNESS

Garth Greenwell is the author of *What Belongs to You*, which won the British Book Award for Debut of the Year, was long-listed for the National Book Award, and was a finalist for six other awards, including the PEN/Faulkner Award and the Los Angeles Times Book Prize. A *New York Times Book Review* Editors' Choice, it was named a Best Book of 2016 by more than fifty publications in nine countries, and is being translated into a dozen languages. His fiction has appeared in the *New Yorker*, the *Paris Review*, and *A Public Space*, and he has written nonfiction for the *Guardian*, the *London Review of Books*, and *Harper's Magazine*. He lives in Iowa City.

CLEANNESS

Garth Greenwell

PICADOR

First published 2020 by Farrar, Straus and Giroux

First published in the UK in paperback 2020 by Picador
an imprint of Pan Macmillan
The Smithson, 6 Briset Street, London EC1M 5NR
Associated companies throughout the world
www.panmacmillan.com

ISBN 978-1-5098-7464-4

3 5 7 9 8 6 4 2

A CIP catalogue record for this book is available from the British Library.

Printed and bound by CPI Group (UK) Ltd, Croydon, CR0 4YY

Visit **www.picador.com** to read more about all our books
and to buy them. You will also find features, author interviews and
news of any author events, and you can sign up for e-newsletters
so that you're always first to hear about our new releases.

For Dimiter Kenarov

CONTENTS

I.

II. LOVING R.

III.

I

MENTOR

We had agreed to meet at the fountain in front of the McDonald's in Slaveykov Square. By my American standards G. was late, and as I waited for him I browsed the book stalls the square is famous for, their wares piled high under awnings in front of the city library. Really it wasn't a fountain anymore, it had been shuttered for years, since faulty wiring stopped a man's heart one summer as he dipped his fingers into the cool water there. It was December now, though winter hadn't yet really taken hold; the sun was out and the weather was mild, it wasn't unpleasant to stand for a bit and browse the books on display. From the beginning of the year G. had caught my attention, at first simply because he was beautiful, and then for the special quality of friendship I thought I saw between him and another boy in my class, the intensity with which G. sought him out and the privacy he drew about them. It was familiar to me, that intensity, a story from my own adolescence, as was the basking ambivalence with which the other boy received it, how he both invited it and held it off. I had some idea, then, what we would talk about, and why school didn't offer enough secrecy for us to talk about it there, but I was still curious: he wasn't a student I was particularly close to, he didn't stop by my room outside of class, he had never confided in me or sought me out, and I wondered what crisis was bringing him to me now.

I was getting annoyed with the booksellers who, sensing my foreignness, kept directing me to their piles of battered American paperbacks, and as G. continued not to appear I wondered if my sacrificed afternoon would go to waste. But then he did appear, standing beside me suddenly, and my annoyance dissolved at the sight of him. He stood out here, with his slightly formal clothes, his feathered hair, though in the States he would have been generic enough, an East Coast aspirant prep school kid, maybe not quite the real thing, especially if he smiled too broadly (as he was careful almost never to do) and revealed a lower set of teeth in un-American disarray. He was friendly enough in greeting me, but as always there was something reserved about him, as if he were deciding whether or not to pronounce a judgment he was on the point of making. He asked me where we should go only to dismiss all my proposals, saying he would take me to a favorite place of his own, and then he set off, walking not beside but in front of me, preventing conversation and as if he were ready to deny any association with me at all. I was hardly a newcomer, I had lived in Sofia for two years, but I had remained a kind of dilettante of the city, and soon—though the center is small and we hadn't gone far from Slaveykov and Graf Ignatiev, the part of it I knew best—I had no idea where we were. My ignorance wasn't for lack of trying: for months after I arrived, I came to the center every morning I could, walking the streets as the city woke up and returning to mark off my route on a map pinned to the wall. And yet those same streets, even a short time later, seemed almost entirely unfamiliar; I could never understand how they fit together, and only the stray detail (an old cornice carving, an oddly painted façade) reminded me I had passed that way before. Walking behind G., as always when I was with someone born in Sofia, I had a sense of the city opening itself up, the monolithic blank concrete of the Soviet-style apartment blocks giving way to unsuspected courtyards and cafés and paths through overgrown little parks. As we entered these spaces, which were quieter and less traveled than the boulevards, G. slowed his pace, allowing me to come up beside him, and we walked in a more companionable way, though still without speaking.

It was in one of these courtyards or little parks that G.'s restaurant was hidden. It was below ground, and as we approached the door that would take us down to it, I noticed a neighboring storefront, an antiquarian shop, its windows crowded with icons—Cyril and Methodius, a beatific Mary, St. George on horseback hooking the dragon through the mouth—as well as Nazi paraphernalia, watches and billfolds and flasks all stamped with a broken cross. These are common at antiques shops and outdoor markets here, souvenirs for tourists or for young men longing for a time when they might have allied themselves, however disastrously, with some real power in the world. The space we descended into was larger than I had expected, an open room with booths along each side and, at the back, a bar I imagined crowded at night with university students. The room was lit by a row of small windows near the top of one wall, their panes clouded and stained with smoke, so that the light was strangely muted, as if steeped in tea. G. gestured toward one of the booths, most of which were empty, and we sat down in it together.

G. laid his cigarettes on the table and rested the tips of his fingers on the pack, tapping it lightly. I realized that he was waiting for permission, that even though nearly everyone in the restaurant was smoking already, he wouldn't join them unless I gave him my approval first. I smiled at him or nodded and he snatched them up, smiling back as if in apology for his eagerness, and the edges of him softened as he took a first long drag. We spoke a little then, pleasantries mostly and the obligatory questions about college; applications had been sent out and the students were waiting to hear back, and though we were all sick of talking about it, it was the subject we all returned to. Fine, he said, it's fine, I'm just waiting, and he said that most of the schools he had applied to were in the States, though many students here now look to the EU, where tuition is cheaper and where they have a better chance of being allowed to stay after they graduate. But that conversation was like a cloth already wrung dry, and soon we were sitting in silence. I brought up poetry then; not long before we had read some American poets of the midcentury, and G.'s own poems in response had been a genuine surprise, witty and fluent, revealing depths his other work had never suggested. One of them especially had impressed me, a poem full of the everyday: descriptions of our school, of his classmates and teachers; and also of a sense that in the world he described there was nowhere he could feel at home. It seemed like a kind of invitation, and I suspected that my response to it, excited and full of encouragement, had invited in turn this meeting.

He pulled a few pages from his bag and slid them toward me, saying Here, I've been working more on these. I was disappointed to see the slightest of the poems he had given me on top, a generic hymn to a feminine ideal, full of exaggerated praise and capitalized pronouns. It was the same draft I had seen already, the page full of my corrections and suggestions, advice I feel obligated to give even unpromising student work. You corrected so much, he said, but you didn't correct the most important mistake. I looked down at the page and then up again, confused; I don't see it, I said, what did I miss? He leaned across the table, reaching his arms toward the page so that his upper body rested on the lacquered wood, a peculiarly teenage gesture, I thought, I remembered making it but hadn't made it for years, and he pressed his finger to the margin of the page. Here, he said, pointing to a line where the single word *She* appeared, I made it here and it happens several times, the pronouns are all wrong, and even in his half-prone posture I could see that his whole body was tense. Ah, I said, looking up at him from the page, I see, and then he leaned quickly back, as if released by something, and as though after his revelation he wanted to reassert some space between us. I leaned back too, and pushed the pages across to him again; it was clear that they had served their purpose.

Those poems we read in class, he said then, I had never seen anything like them, I didn't know anything like them existed. He was talking about Frank O'Hara, I understood, whose poems had shocked most of my students, as I intended them to. I had never read anything before, he went on, I mean a story or a poem, that seemed like it was about me, that I could have written it. He didn't look at me as he said this, looking instead at his hands, both of which were on the table in front of him and in one of which a cigarette had shrunk almost to its nub between two fingers. I felt two things as he spoke, first my usual dismay when talking to gay men here, who were more excluded than I had been, growing up in the American south, where at least I had found books that, even if they were always tragic, offered a certain beauty as compensation. But in addition to dismay I felt satisfaction or pride at having provided (as I thought of it) some degree of solace, and maybe this was the bigger part of what I felt. I had gathered him up, I thought, and this sparked a sense of warmth that started in the central pit of me and then radiated out. It was a craftsman's pride, I suppose: I had worked hard to find the right poems for the students, choosing O'Hara for his subject matter but primarily for his joy, his freedom from guardedness and guilt, which would only have reinforced what many of my students already believed about that category or class of people of which I was a part. My satisfaction only deepened when G. continued, after our coffee arrived and we took a moment to add sugar and milk. You're the only person I know who talks about it, who's so public and who isn't ashamed, he said; it's good that you're that way, it must be hard here. This was a kind of acknowledgment one hardly ever hears, and it recalled the sense of mission I had had when I first started teaching, which had faded so decisively since. And again this had the effect of increasing the distance between us, so that even as I saw he remained agitated, tense and anxious, that he was miserable with something he still had to say, I was suffused with a sense of accomplishment, a peculiar and sharp pleasure.

I asked whether there was something else, besides the poems we had read, that made him want to talk to me now. I don't know, he said, I just had to talk to someone, and he twisted his coffee cup slowly in circles as he spoke, the handle passing from one palm to the other. You don't know what it's like, he said, speaking my name, which startled me a little, I'm not sure why, making me feel again—just for a moment and like a kind of echo—how shocking it had been, years before, when my students first called me by my surname. It was so alien then, so little connected to who I was, though now it feels inevitable, the self I have become, perhaps, a diminished self, as it sometimes seems. You don't know what it's like, he went on, there's no one I can talk to, it's impossible here, and he catalogued for me the sources of comfort unavailable to him, his parents, his friends, the adults at school who, in the States, might have been turned to for support; and of course there were no public resources here, no community centers or networks he could seek out. What about online, I said, couldn't you find people there, and he looked up at me sharply. Is that what you think I want, he asked, to meet someone online? I'm not interested in that, he said, and I realized from his tone that he had misunderstood me, that he thought I was suggesting hookup sites, when in fact I had something altogether different in mind, forums and chat rooms of which there are so many in America. But he seemed exasperated by this, too, making a little motion of dismissal with his hands. What good would that do, he said, I live here, not in America, and it's impossible to live here. Besides, and here he leaned away from me again, resting his weight on the padded back of our booth, I've seen some of those sites, he said, I've seen what they talk about, television and pop songs and sex, do you think I have anything to say to them? There's nothing for me there, he said, that's not the life I want, that's not what I want to be. And then, after a pause, Is that what all of them are like, he asked, leaning forward again, is that what it means to be this way? My confidence faltered at this; I had said the wrong thing, and now I felt myself under attack, or anyway drawn more decisively within the compass of his scorn. He knew nothing about me, about those aspects of my life there's no reason for my students to guess at, even though I'm more open than is usual for my vocation, or for my trade, rather, though maybe it was a vocation once. He knew nothing about me, nothing about the appetites that sometimes shame me, and yet still I felt indicted, so that Of course not, I said much more sharply than I should have, and then clamped down on myself before I could say anything more. He drew back when I spoke, and I was sorry for what I had done. I put both of my hands around the cup in front of me, taking a deep breath as I pressed my palms against what warmth was left, and then, when I could speak more calmly, What is the life you want, I asked.

He hunched his shoulders a little, as if to say I don't know or maybe what does it matter, and then he started talking about something else, or what seemed like something else, making me feel again that I was on the wrong tack, that I had failed to sense or say what I should. You know those

poems you put up in the classroom, he began, and I nodded, of course I did: five student poems from the two classes
of twelfth-graders I taught, which I hung up in a little display on the back wall. For a week before the students handed
them in there had been an extraordinary wind in Sofia, fierce
and incessant, a wind from Africa, people said, which played
havoc through the city and left all of us feeling anxious or ex-
alted. It was constant, unignorable, and in each of the poems
I posted it appeared, in one as a snake, in another as horses
galloping on sand, in a third as the sea they galloped by, the
pages hanging on the wall together like panes of a compound
eye. Four of the poems you put up were by me and my closest friends, he said, three of us are in one class and the fourth
is in the other; we hadn't talked about it at all, it was funny
that we wrote about the same thing. Did you know we were
so close, he asked, but I didn't know; I was embarrassed to
realize, in fact, that in the weeks since the assignment I had
forgotten exactly whose work I had chosen, and as G. spoke
that afternoon I would puzzle out only slowly who the
other students in his story were. Or maybe it wasn't funny,
he went on, I guess there's nothing so funny about it, but it
was odd, anyway, how we were all drawn to the same thing.
They had been friends since they came to the College, he said
then, they met as eighth-graders, three boys and one girl, and
almost from the first day they were inseparable. As he spoke
of these friends, I felt that despite my missteps he had decided I was worthy of his confidence, of a deeper confidence
than he had already shown; or maybe it wasn't judgment but
need that drove him to speak to me as he did, not for some
virtue of my own but merely for the function I could serve.

They were easy with one another in a way he had never been before, he told me, he had never been part of a group like that; he had always held himself apart from others, it was his nature to hold himself apart. I felt lucky, he said, I expected the whole time that I would mess it up, that our friendship would burn out the way my friendships always burn out; I don't have any friends from before the College, he said, they slip away from me somehow. Or maybe those weren't the phrases he used, burn out and slip away, maybe I've supplied them just now, though I'm fairly certain of the shape of what he said as we sipped our second cups of coffee, as I kept pouring more sugar into mine, packet after packet. But they didn't slip away, he continued, they stuck. We met at the same place every morning before classes and then again for lunch, after school we took the bus together, on weekends we went to the park or the mall. Even during vacations we were together, we went to the mountains for winter break and spent summer at the seaside, our families became friends, we all traveled together. They're not like me, they had lots of friends, they've always been popular, but we were still a special group, I always had my place. I had what I wanted, for the first time I didn't want anything else, do you understand, and I nodded; I understood him entirely, and it seemed to me the intimacy he had drawn between us deepened further, becoming a sort of kinship, which I greeted with both welcome and dread.

There were more people in the restaurant now, and G. lowered his voice as the booths around us filled and the air grew thick with smoke. I was leaning forward to hear him, and it occurred to me that he had brought me here for the added privacy of it, the privacy of the booth and his lowered voice but also the privacy of the language; at any of the brighter cafés on the boulevards we would have heard English but here no one else was speaking it, we were alone in that way too. I didn't think of B. as special then, not really, he said, speaking of the boy who was also in my class, whom I thought of as G.'s particular friend; we were all equally friends, the four of us, but B. and I had always been in the same classes, in eighth and ninth grade, and then the next year they put us in different sections. It shouldn't have mattered, he said, we were good students, we didn't talk in class or fool around, and we still had our time together as a group. But it did matter, he said, I couldn't stand it. I made them switch me, I said that I hated the other students, I said they were cruel to me. It wasn't true but I made my mother believe it, I made her come to the school to complain, and after a few days they put me where I wanted to be. Everything should have been fine then but it wasn't fine, I knew that it shouldn't have made me so upset, I couldn't understand why it had. But that's not true, he said, shaking his head just slightly, I did understand, at least a little, I knew I felt something I shouldn't feel.

He lit another cigarette. For some time as he spoke he hadn't been smoking, but now he took a deep drag and again I saw him relax as he exhaled. But really everything was fine, he said, I still had my place with my friends and I still had my friendship with B., I could do without the rest of it. B. dated a few girls, so did I, and it didn't mean much more to him than to me, we were still the same thing to each other, all four of us, and now for the first time G. named the third member of the group, the female friend, what he had said

about her to that point hadn't been enough for me to be sure
who she was. She was a beautiful girl, smart, kind, one of my
favorite students; she was undemanding, by which I mean
that she had never been a source of the worry that makes up
so much of teaching, she was a student you could be sure of.
Everything was fine, he said again, and this year was our big
year, we were finally seniors. We'd been looking forward to
it for so long, the trips we would take, the parties. There was
a tradition of these celebrations, I knew, one each quarter and
then a final post-prom bacchanalia at the seaside that lasted,
for some of them, until they left for university in the fall.

We arranged to rent a house together for the fall trip, he
said, close enough to the others to join the parties at night but
far enough away to have the days to ourselves. We were in
the mountains, in a little village that's empty most of the year,
there was nothing else for kilometers around. We brought
everything with us, alcohol, music, even little lights to hang
up in one of the houses so we could dance. There was a deck
that looked out over the mountain, and on the first night we
sat there late, talking and drinking, laughing in a way I only
ever laughed when I was with them. It was a perfect night,
he said, with the long weekend still stretching before them,
when have I ever been so happy. There came over his face at
this an expression of such longing I had to look away. I had
been feeling this increasingly as he spoke, this desire to look
away, and had resisted it, wanting him to know I was listening, that I was ready to receive whatever he offered; and this
was all the more true because he so seldom looked at me,
staring instead at the table, at his hands or the empty cup
between them. I wanted to be present when he did look, I

wanted him to see my attention, which was my way of catching him, I suppose, or that's what I wanted it to be, I wanted
to gather him up. But as he continued to speak I failed even
at this, I was unable to keep my eyes on his face.

I went to bed before B., he said then, we were sharing a
room but he wanted to stay up a bit and I was exhausted.
I thought he would wake me up when he came in, that we
would talk for a little like we always did, just a few minutes
the two of us by ourselves; but I slept through the night and
when I woke his side of the bed was untouched. I thought
maybe he had fallen asleep out on the deck, but it had gotten cold in the night and there was nobody outside. It was
early, foggy and quiet, like it only ever is in the mountains,
and I stood for a while at the wooden rail, looking down at
the village where everything was still. He waited for them in
the main room, doing nothing, he said, just waiting until he
heard a noise on the upper floor and then the final member
of their group came down. G. called this boy by name and
for the first time I had a clear sense of the four of them, all
of them students I had seen every day, more or less, with so
little idea of what passed between them. I have such a strange
perspective on their lives; in one sense I see them as no one
else sees them, my profession is a kind of long looking, and
in another they are entirely opaque to me. He was so excited, G. said of this fourth friend, he couldn't wait to tell me
about the night before, how after I went to bed they stayed
up drinking, how there was something going on between B.
and our other friend, how they began talking to each other
as though he weren't there, until finally he said good night
and left them alone. And then, before he fell asleep he heard

them walk past his door together. Isn't it great, this friend said to G., they're perfect for each other, and it's been coming for so long; he couldn't understand how it hadn't happened already, it was so obviously what they wanted. And he said all this to me like I knew it already, G. went on, like it was so clear it didn't need to be said. But I didn't know, I hadn't seen anything, and as I sat there I felt something I had never felt before, it was like I was falling into something, like water though it wasn't really like water, it was like a new element, G. said. But surely he didn't say precisely that, surely this is something I've added; added in solidarity, I'd like to say, but it wasn't solidarity I felt as I listened to him, it was more like the laying of a claim. The experience he had had was my own, I felt, I recognized it exactly, and as he spoke I felt myself falling also, into his story and his feeling both, I was trapped in what he told.

Finally we heard them moving, G. went on, we heard a door closing and steps coming from above, and then they came down the stairs together. They were shy, holding hands, it was like they were nervous about us seeing them. Our friend whistled at them and laughed, clapping his hands, and then they all laughed together. But I couldn't laugh with them, not really, I could only pretend to laugh. They had changed, the two of them, they seemed like different people sitting there in chairs they pulled together as close as they could, leaning against each other, like people I didn't know; and even though I could see B. glancing at me now and again, I couldn't make myself meet his eyes. G. paused, lighting another cigarette though the ashtray was already full. The restaurant was busy now, every table was taken, the room was loud with conversation and laughter, but G. hadn't raised his voice as he spoke; I had to strain to hear him, leaning forward as best I could. He was silent for a while, dragging on his cigarette. I was grateful for the pause, I was exhausted by listening to him, by the effort of it in that noisy space but also by the obligation it imposed, not just to listen but to feel in a way I had grown unaccustomed to feel. I didn't want him to keep talking, I knew what he would say; it was such an ordinary story, which was what I had tried to tell myself when I was young and felt what G. felt now. But for G. it wasn't a story at all, it was the air he breathed, though it was even less like air than water, it was the opposite of air.

Over the next weeks I lost all the pleasure I had ever taken in my friends, he said. B. told me about every minute of it, every feeling, and I hated him while he spoke, I hated his happiness. There was so much to feel, G. said, I had never let myself imagine what I wanted, I had never in all those years fantasized about him, not once; I hardly fantasized about anything, I didn't want that part of me to exist. But now he was all I could think about, I couldn't concentrate in my classes—and it was true, I thought, I had noticed it, the abstraction, the missed work, the fact that so often I caught him staring off into space and had to call him back from wherever he had gone. Every day I saw something I couldn't stand, G. said, the two of them kissing or holding hands, they were so happy together. Everything I had looked forward to was ruined, the year was ruined, and I was lonely in a way I had never been before, not just alone but incapable of being not alone, do you understand? I looked up at him, having heard the grimace I saw now on his face, a look of such desolation I barely caught myself before I reached for him, wanting to place my hand on his, though I had been teaching long enough to know never to touch students, or almost never, even innocent touches can be suspect. And he wouldn't have welcomed it, I thought, he wasn't the type to want it, it would have been an intrusion. But maybe I was wrong, maybe it was precisely what he wanted, maybe it was some better or wiser part of me I restrained. That's the worst thing about teaching, that our actions either have no force at all or have force beyond all intention, and not only our actions but our failures to act, gestures and words held back or unspoken, all we might have done and failed to do; and, more than this, that the consequences echo across years and silence, we can never really know what we've done.

G. was quiet for a moment, keeping his eyes on the table. When I told him, he went on, it was by accident, almost, I told him all at once and without any plan. We were alone for the first time in weeks, out of the city, at a house my parents keep up on Vitosha. I knew the area he meant, I thought, a band of exclusive neighborhoods built up the side of the mountain, each year climbing farther up; it was just a half-hour drive from Sofia but it was like a different world, with its own climate free of the congestion and noise of the center. This was a few weeks ago, he said, we had gone up on a Friday for a quick trip, we were coming back on Saturday. But we planned to spend the whole day there, and it was still morning, and it had been a wonderful night. G. was quiet for a while, and then, What was I thinking, he said, speaking to himself more than to me. He had waved the waitress away when she approached, the cups in front of us were empty and cold. G. had his cigarettes but I was empty-handed, and suddenly I felt that I should make some gesture of comfort or encouragement, though I wasn't sure how much encouragement I wanted to give. I had heard enough of his story, I wanted to leave the restaurant and the thick air that made my eyes and my throat ache, I wanted him to stop talking, I wanted to go home.

I don't know, G. said, answering his own question, I wanted it to end, I guess, I didn't want to go back to being so miserable; or maybe it was something else, maybe I did have some hope, not that he would feel what I felt but that he would let me give it to him somehow, that he would receive it. If I could just kiss him, he said, his voice stripped now and small, if I could kiss him just once, that would be enough, I wouldn't want anything more. I looked at him then, wondering if he meant what he said, if he was really so new to desire that he could believe it. I don't think so, I said, speaking for the first time since he had started his story, my voice raw, I don't think that's how it works; it was a ridiculous thing to say, I knew it even as I spoke. Whatever, G. said, still not looking up, it doesn't matter, he didn't give me a chance. I told him that I loved him but he didn't understand me, or he pretended not to understand, I had to explain it, and once I started speaking I couldn't stop, after being silent for so long I spoke too much. But it didn't matter what I said, I only made things worse by talking. He didn't welcome it at all, and he hadn't had any idea; I guess I thought he had known it somehow, that he was all I thought about, the only thing, the only thing I cared about. But he was surprised, really surprised, and he didn't welcome it, he turned away when I kept talking. He wasn't cruel to me, he was gentle, he was even kind, but he didn't pretend we could go on as we had. We would stop being friends, he said, he said he was sorry; he didn't want me to suffer, and it was the quickest way to end suffering, and anyway he couldn't be comfortable with me now. I was crying then, G. said, I don't think he had ever seen me cry before, I couldn't stop. Why did you tell me, he said, I've lost something too, you've taken something from me too. And I had, I realized, I had ruined so much, for him and for me. I was wrong to tell him, G. said, I shouldn't have said anything, along with everything else now I'm so sorry for what I said. But there's nothing I can do, I have to live with it, like I have to live with everything else I feel. He paused, and then, But what if I can't bear it, he said, looking up at me, finally catching my eye, and though at first I thought the question was rhetorical I realized it was genuine, I needed to have something to say. I remembered the confidence I had had, hours before, in my own competence, the pleasure I had taken in the solace I could give, and I wished I could have some of it back, that it would ease the sense I had now of helplessness and loss, though loss of what I wasn't precisely sure, an idea of myself, I suppose, which shouldn't have been so precious to me but was.

Other people have gone through this, I began, finding it difficult to speak. Other people have felt it, they bear it and they get through it, they aren't trapped in it forever. These feelings, I said lamely, all of them, they will get easier, they'll stop being the only thing you feel, they'll fade and make room for other feelings. And then, in time, you'll look at them from far away, almost entirely without pain, as if they were felt by somebody else, or felt in a dream. That's what it's like, I said, thinking I had struck on something, it's precisely like waking from a dream, and like a self in a dream the self that feels this will be incomprehensible to you, and the intensity you feel now will be like a puzzle you can't solve, a puzzle it finally isn't worth your while to solve. I was speaking of myself, of course, of my own experience with love, with overwhelming love that had made me at times such a stranger to myself. But I could see this failing even as I spoke, I could see him recoiling from me, looking at me with an expression first of surprise and then of dismay, and then of something like revulsion. I don't want to feel it less, he said, I don't want it to stop, I don't want it to seem like it wasn't real. It would all be for nothing if that happened, he said, I don't want it to be a dream, I want it to be real, all of it. And who else could I love, he asked, his voice softening, we grew up together, in the same country, with the same language, we became adults together; who could I meet wherever I go next who could know me like that, who could love me as much as he could love me, who could I love as much? What life could I want except for that life, he said, reminding me of the question I had asked so long before, he hadn't forgotten it, his whole recitation had been an answer, what other life than that could I bear?

He raised his hand then, signaling for the waitress and signaling too that our talk was over, that he had exhausted all hope of my helpfulness; and I was both relieved and exasperated by this, and exasperated too by what he had said. But this is a story you're telling yourself, I said, a story you've made up that will make you unhappy. There's nothing inevitable about it, it's a choice you've made, you can choose a different story. But he was already gone, though he was still with me at the table; he was taking out his wallet to pay the check, which I covered with my hand as the waitress laid it down. I've got it, I said, and he thanked me, for the coffee and for the talk, as he said. He stood up and put on his coat while I was still counting out bills, and though he stood there willing to wait for me he was clearly relieved when I let him go, saying I would wait for my change. I watched him as he left, walking hunched over just slightly, carrying away the despair he held on to so tightly, and I told myself he would grow out from under it, that he would go to university and discover a new life in England or America, new freedoms and possibilities, a greater scope for love, and with it room in himself for other feelings. The pain he felt now would become a story he told to others, I thought, and of course he couldn't believe this, of course it seemed impossible, I told myself, of course I had failed to make him see it.

I walked into the street, breathing in the fresh air and setting off in what I hoped was the direction of the Nevsky Cathedral, from which I was sure I could find my way home. As I walked I remembered other times I had felt impatience or exasperation with my students' private lives, with their outsized passions and griefs, and I felt this even as I knew that the perspective they lacked couldn't be willed, that it came only and inevitably with time. He would be all right, I thought again, comforting myself by thinking it, though I thought too that he wasn't altogether mistaken in what he had said, that there would be loss in loving another, that the perspective that limited his grief would also limit his love, which, having taken the measure of its bounds, he could never again imagine as boundless. And I had thought this before, too, how much we lose in gaining this truer vision of ourselves, the vision I had urged upon my student, the vision it was my obligation to urge, though it carried us away from our dreams of ourselves, from the grandeur of novels and poems which it was also my obligation to impart. How much smaller I have become, I said to myself, through an erosion necessary to survival perhaps and perhaps still to be regretted, I've worn myself down to a bearable size. And then I realized that I had wandered into a maze of narrow streets, the walls on either side too high to glimpse the gold dome of my landmark, and I began to walk more quickly, spurred by the unease that always claims me when I lose track of where I am.

GOSPODAR

It would have made me laugh in English, I think, the word he used for himself and that he insisted I use for him—not that he had had to insist, of course, I would call him whatever he wanted. It was the word for master or lord, but in his language it had a resonance it would have lacked in my own, partaking equally of the everyday (*Gospodine*, my students say in greeting, mister or sir) and of the scented chant of the cathedral. He was naked when he opened the door, backlit in the entrance of his apartment, or naked except for a series of leather straps that crossed his chest, serving no particular function; and this too might have made me laugh, were there not something in his manner that forbade it. He didn't greet me or invite me in, but turned without a word and walked to the center of what I took to be the apartment's main room. I didn't follow him, I waited at the edge of the light until he turned again and faced me, and then he did speak, telling me to undress in the hallway. Take off everything, he said, take off everything and then come in.

I was surprised by this, which was a risk for him as for me, for him more than for me, since he was surrounded by neighbors any of whom might open their doors. He lived on a middle floor of one of the huge apartment blocks that stand everywhere in Sofia like fortresses or keeps, ugly and imperious, though this is a false impression they give, they're so poorly built as already to be crumbling away. I obeyed him, I took off my shoes and then my coat and began to undo the long line of buttons on my shirt, my hands fumbling in the dark and in my excitement, too. I pulled down my pants, awkward in my haste, wanting him and also wanting to end my exposure, though it was part of my excitement. It was for this excitement I had come, something to draw me out of the grief I still felt for R.; he had left months before, long enough for grief to have passed but it hadn't passed, and I found myself resorting again to habits I thought I had escaped, though that's the wrong word for it, escaped, given the eagerness with which I returned to them.

I made a bundle of my clothes, balling my pants and shirt and underthings in my coat, and I held this in one hand and my shoes in the other and stood, still not entering, my skin bristling both from cold and from that profounder exposure I felt. *Ne ne, kuchko*, he said, using for the first time the word that would be his only name for me. It's our word, bitch, an exact equivalent, but he spoke it almost tenderly, as if in fondness; no, he said, fold your clothes nicely before you come in, be a good girl. At this last something rose up in me, as at a step too far in humiliation. Most men would feel this, I think, especially men like me, who are taught that it's the worst thing, to seem like a woman; when I was a boy my father responded to any sign of it with a viciousness out of all proportion, as though he might keep me from what I would become, a faggot, as he said, which remained his word for me when for all his efforts I found myself as I am. Something rose up in me at what he said, this man who still barred my way, and then it lay back down, and I folded my clothes neatly and stepped inside, closing the door behind me.

It was a comfortless room. There was an armoire of some sort, a table, a plush chair, all from an earlier era. These spaces are passed from generation to generation; people can spend their whole lives amid the same objects and their evidence of other lives, as almost never happens in my own country, or never anymore. And yet it was impossible to imagine friends or family gathering there. I stood for a moment just in front of the door, and then the man told me to kneel. I could feel him looking at me in the clinical light, inspecting or evaluating me, and when he spoke it was as if with distaste. *Mnogo si debel*, he said, you're very fat, and I looked down at myself, at my thighs and the flesh folded over them, the flesh I have hated my entire life, and though I remained silent, I thought Not so very fat. It was part of our contract, that he could say such things and I would endure them. I wasn't as fat as he was, anyway: he was larger in person than in the photos he had sent, as you come to expect, larger and older, too; he was as old as my father, or almost, anyway nearer to him than to me. But he stood there as though free of both vanity and shame, with an indifference that seemed absolute and, in my experience of such things, unique. Even very beautiful men are eager to be admired, wherever you touch them they harden their muscles, turning their best angles to the light;

but he seemed to feel no concern at all for my response to him, and it was then that I felt the first stirrings of unease.

He neither spoke nor gestured, and the longer he appraised me, the more I feared that having come all this way I would be told to leave. It wasn't the lost time I would resent, but the waste of the anticipation that had mounted in me over the several days I had chatted with him online, an anticipation that wasn't exactly desire, as it wasn't desire that I felt now, though I was hard, though I had been hard even as I climbed the stairs, even in the taxi that had brought me there. He was an unhandsome man, though in the way of some older men he seemed solid in his corpulence, thick through the chest and arms. His face was blunt-featured, generic somehow; it was clear that he had never been attractive, or rather that his primary attraction had always been the bearing he had either been born with or had cultivated, the pose of uncaring that seemed to draw all value into itself, that seemed entirely self-sufficient. He would never be called a faggot, I thought, whatever the nature of his desires.

Then, to my relief, *Ela tuka* he said, come here, having decided to keep me, at least for a while. When I began to rise he snapped *Dolu*, stay down, and I moved across the space on all fours, the carpet featureless and gray and coarse. When I reached him he took my hair in his hand and lifted me up onto my knees, not roughly, maybe just as a means of communication more efficient than speech. I had told him I wasn't Bulgarian in one of our online chats, warning him that when we met there might be things I wouldn't understand, but he had asked none of the usual questions, he seemed not to care why I had come to his country, where so few come and fewer still stay long enough to learn the language, which is spoken nowhere else, which even here, as the country shrinks, is spoken by fewer people each day; it's not difficult to imagine it disappearing altogether, the language and the country both. We'll understand each other, he had said, don't worry, and maybe it was just to ensure this understanding that he had taken me in hand, firmly but not painfully guiding me to my knees.

He let go of my hair then, freeing his hand to move down the side of my face, almost stroking it before he cupped it in his palm. It was a tender gesture, and his voice was tender too as he said *Kuchko*, addressing me as if solicitously and tilting my head so that we gazed at each other face to face; his fingers flexed against my cheek, almost in a caress. I leaned my head into him, resting it on his palm as he spoke again in that tone of tenderness or solicitude, Tell me, *kuchko*, tell me what you want. And I did tell him, at first slowly and with the usual words, reciting the script that both does and does not express my desires; and then I spoke more quickly and more searchingly, drawn forward by the tone of his voice, what seemed like tenderness although it was not tenderness, until I found myself suddenly in some recess or depth where I had never been. There were things I could say in his language, because I spoke it poorly, without self-consciousness or shame, as if there were something in me unreachable in my own language, something I could reach only with that blunter instrument by which I too was made a blunter instrument, and I found myself at last at the end of my strange litany saying again and again I want to be nothing, I want to be nothing. Good, the man said, good, speaking with the same tenderness and smiling a little as he cupped my face in his palm and bent forward, bringing his own face to mine, as if to kiss me, I thought, which surprised me though I would have welcomed it. Good, he said a third time, his hand letting go of my cheek and taking hold of my hair again, forcing my neck farther back, and then suddenly and with great force he spat into my face.

He pulled me forward, still holding my hair, and pressed my face hard into his crotch, hard enough that it must have been as uncomfortable for him as for me; any pleasure we took would be an accident, or a consequence of some other aim. Which isn't to say that I didn't feel pleasure; I had never stopped being hard, and when he said to me Breathe me in, smell me, I did so eagerly, taking great gasps. I had felt it before, too, when he spat on me it was like a spark along the track of my spine, who knows why we take pleasure in such things, maybe it's best not to look into it too closely. He was feeling it too, I could feel his cock thicken against my cheek, then lengthen and lift; there had been no change in it during my long recitation, that catalog of desires I had named, but now at our first real touch he grew hard. He kept one hand at the back of my head, gripping my hair and holding me in place, though there was no need, as surely he knew; but with the other he was reaching for something, as I could tell from the shifts in his balance and weight, and when he pulled me away from him, he slipped it quickly over my head. It was a chain, I realized as I felt it cold against my neck, or rather the kind of leash you use with difficult dogs, and immediately he pulled it tight, letting me feel the pinch of it. This didn't excite me, it was part of the pageantry I was indifferent to, but I didn't object; I assented, though he hadn't sought my permission or consent. And then he took another chain, this one shorter and finer, with little toothed clamps at each end, which (using both his hands, letting the leash fall free, since after all I wasn't an animal, I didn't need to be bound) he attached to my chest. It was the first real pain he had caused me, it made me suck in my breath, but it wasn't too much pain, and not unexciting; a thrill ran through me at this, too, and at what it promised.

Dobre, he said when he had finished, good, though he was speaking of his own work now and not of me. He took up the larger chain again and pulled it tight, twisting his wrist to gather up the slack, which he wrapped around his curled fingers until they were nearly flush against my neck. He was putting me on a short leash, I thought, though I was thinking more of his cock, which I was eager for now, perhaps because of the pain at my chest, which was more than pain, which was excitement too, as was the tightness of the chain around my neck, in which I felt the strength of his arm keeping me from what I wanted. Whatever chemical change desire is had taken hold and I was lit up with it, so that after all I did strain against the leash, he had been right to make it so short. It was a kind of disobedience but a kind he would like, and even as he tightened his grip on the chain I heard him laugh or almost laugh, a slow satisfied chuckle. It was a sound of approval and I glowed with it. She wants something, he said, still chuckling, and he lifted his foot to my crotch, feeling my erection as I knelt before him, she likes it, and then he used his foot to pull my cock down, letting it go so that it snapped back up, making me flinch. Then his foot moved lower and he placed his toes beneath my balls, which he fondled roughly, flexing his ankle until there was not quite pain but an intimation of pain. He was dulling my pleasure, I thought, not removing it entirely but taking off its edge.

But he didn't take off its edge, not really, and when there was a slackening in the leash I lunged forward, like the dog he called me. There wasn't anything special about his cock, it was solid and sizeable and thick, but none of these to a remarkable degree, and he had shaved himself as all men here do, which I hate, the bareness of it is obscene somehow, I can't accustom myself to it. But I was eager, and as I took him in my mouth I felt the gratitude I nearly always feel in such moments, not so much to him as to whatever arrangement of things had allowed me what as a child I thought I would always be denied. It was large enough that I didn't try to take all of it at once; eager as I was there are certain preparations required, the relaxation and lubrication of passages, a general warming up. But immediately his hand was on my head again, forcing me down, and when it was clear that the passage was blocked, he used both of his hands to hold me, at once pulling me to him and jerking his hips forward in short, savage thrusts, saying *Dai gurloto*, give me your throat, an odd construction I had never heard before. This was painful, and not only for me, it must have hurt him too. But I did give my throat, I found an angle that gave him access, and soon enough I relaxed and there was a rush of saliva and he could move however he wanted, as he did for a while, maybe there was pleasure for him after all. As there was for me, the intense pleasure I've never been able to account for, that can't be accounted for mechanically; the pleasure of service, I've sometimes thought, or more darkly the pleasure of being used, the exhilaration of being made an object that had been lacking in sex with R., though that had had its own pleasures, pleasures I longed for but that had in no way compensated for the lack of this. I want to be nothing, I had said to him, and it was a way of being nothing, or next to nothing, a convenience, a tool.

He stopped moving then, taking his hands from my head and even from the chain, which fell superfluous and cold down my back. *Kuchkata*, he said, not *kuchko* anymore, the vocative that had softened the word and made it tender to my ears; no longer addressing me but speaking of the object I had become, he said Let the bitch do it herself. I obeyed it, the order he had spoken not to me but to the air, I forced myself upon him with a violence greater than his own, wanting to please him, I suppose, but that isn't true; I wanted to satisfy myself more than him, or rather to assuage that force or compulsion that drew me to him, that force that can make me such a stranger to myself, it is a failing to be so prone to it but I am prone to it. He let me do this for a while, setting my own pace, and then there came the shift in his balance that meant he was reaching to the table beside him again, choosing some new object. He struck me with it a moment later, not very hard but hard enough that I jerked, interrupting the rhythm I had set, and he placed his hand on my head again, taking hold of me as if I might bolt. It was another prop of the sort I had always laughed at before, a cat-o'-nine-tails, a kind of short whip with several strips of leather hanging down; the one time it had been used on me before, the man had been timid and I had felt nothing at all, except to despise

him a little because he used it only for show. This was something else, and though I had jerked more from shock than
from pain there was pain too, less in the actual blow than in
the moment after, a sharp heat spreading along my back.

He said a word I didn't understand then, which from his
tone I took as something like steady, the kind of mixed reas-
surance and admonishment one might give a startled horse,
and his grip on my head softened, he flexed his fingers again
in that gesture that was almost a caress. I was surprised at
what I felt then, which was outsized and overwhelming, gratitude at what seemed like kindness from this man who had
been so stern; it was something I hadn't felt before, or not
for a very long time. I began moving again, having frozen
at the shock of the first blow, brought back by his caress or
perhaps there had been a very slight pressure from his hand,
I'm not sure. I took the whole length of him, and I felt his
hand rise and fall again, this time more gently, and since I
had warning it didn't interrupt the motion I had fallen into, it
became a part of that motion; we fell into a rhythm together,
and as his strokes grew quicker and more intense so did my
own. Soon enough I was in real pain, my back had grown
tender, and I realized that I had begun making noises, little
whimpers and cries, and they too became part of the rhythm
we had fallen into, his arm rising and falling and my own
movement forward and back, and with that movement the
swinging of the smaller chain at my chest, the ache that had
grown dull but that shifted as I swayed. Then he broke our
rhythm, suddenly pulling me to him and thrusting his hips
forward at the same time, his grip tight, and as he ground
me against him he struck me several times quickly and very

hard, and I cried out with real urgency, an animal objection. But I couldn't cry out, the passage was blocked, and with the effort I began to choke, the mechanism failed and I struggled against him; I tried to wrench my head away, I even brought my hands to his thighs but he held me firm. He struck me five or six times in this way, or maybe seven or eight, they were indistinct as I struggled, moving incoherently, at once pushing myself back from him and flinching at the blows. Then he was still, and though he didn't release me he drew back, letting me breathe and grow calm again. *Dobra kuchka*, he said, again not addressing me but praising me to the air, and his hands were gentle as he held me, not constraining but steadying, a comfort for which I felt again that strange, inappropriate gratitude.

I was cold as I knelt there, I had broken out in a sweat. The man was breathing heavily too, he had exerted himself, the rest was as much for him as for me. He knew what he was doing, I thought with sudden admiration; he knew how far to push and when to ease off, and I was excited at the thought of being taken further by him, into territories I had only glimpsed or had intimations of. Then, still keeping one hand on my head, he reached down and very quickly removed first one and then the other clamp from my chest, at which there was a quick flare of pain, making me cry out again, and then a flood of extraordinary pleasure, not sexual pleasure exactly but something like euphoria, a lifting and lightness and unsteadiness, as with certain drugs. He returned his hand to my head and gripped me firmly again, still not moving, having grown very still; even his cock had softened just slightly, it was large but more giving in my mouth. And then he repeated the word I didn't know but that I thought meant steady and suddenly my mouth was filled with warmth, bright and bitter, his urine, which I took as I had taken everything else, it was a kind of pride in me to take it. *Kuchko*, he said as I drank, speaking softly and soothingly, addressing me again, *mnogo si dobra*, you're very good, and he said this a second time and a third before he was done.

He stepped back, withdrawing from my mouth, and told me to lay myself out on the gray carpet face down, with my arms stretched over my head. It was a difficult position, the carpet was rough and there was no good place for my cock, which was still hard, having never softened, or softened only briefly, though we had been together I thought for a long time. He grunted as he knelt beside me, settling his large frame, and then he placed his hands on my back, not stroking or kneading but appraising. *Mnogo si debel*, he said again, you're very fat, pinching my flesh between his fingers, but I like you, he said, *haresvash mi*, you're pleasing to me, and I thanked him, I said *radvam se*, I'm glad of that, though a more literal translation would be something like I rejoice or take joy in it, which was closer to what I felt. His hands moved lower then, to my ass and the opening there, which he touched, still tenderly, though I flinched as he tested it, he said How is your hole and inched the tip of one dry finger inside. *Kuchko*, he said again, and again I like you, still speaking tenderly to me, so that I felt I had passed some test, that I had proven myself and entered within the scope of his affection, or if not his affection at least his regard. Then he stretched out beside me, not quite touching me, and brought his face close to mine as his hand moved lower still, between my legs, which I spread slightly before lifting up my hips to let his hand snake between my legs and touch my cock for the first time. And you like me too, he said, feeling how hard I was; he gripped me tightly before letting me go. Very much, I said, I like you very much, and it was true, I was excited by him in a new way, or almost new; I had never been with anyone so skilled or so patient. His hand was on my balls now, which he drew together and down, making a kind of ring with his thumb and forefinger, drawing them tighter before folding the rest of his hand around them. He wasn't hurting me yet but I grew tense anyway, and he sensed this, bringing his forehead to my temple, laying it there and whispering again that I was good. And then he began to tighten his grip, very slowly and with a steady pressure on all sides, causing that terrible low ache to build in my abdomen, and I pressed my own forehead into the coarse fabric of the carpet, rubbing it very slightly back and forth. I groaned as he continued to squeeze, and then gasped as I felt his tongue on my cheek, a broad swipe from my jaw to my temple. *Mozhesh*, he said, you can take it, and then I cried out when suddenly he squeezed me harder and let me go.

Good, he said again, whispering with his forehead still pressed to my temple, as I lay there recovering, though the worst thing about that particular pain is that you recover so slowly; the pain welled instead of ebbing, settling in my groin and the pit of my stomach and the backs of my thighs. When his weight shifted next to me I almost protested, I almost said *chakaite*, wait, I had even taken the breath to say it. But he hushed me, making a soothing sound to keep me in my place as he shifted his frame over mine, sliding himself over until he was resting on top of me. It helped, the weight of him, it pressed me down and pressed down the pain I still felt, that ache about which there is nothing erotic, or not for me. I know there are men who like it, who go to great lengths to find others who will hurt them in exactly this way, though I've never been able to fathom the pleasure they take from it. But then there's no fathoming pleasure, the forms it takes or their sources, nothing we can imagine is beyond it; however far beyond the pale of our own desires, for someone it is the intensest desire, the key to the latch of the self, or the promised key, a key that perhaps never turns. It's what I love most about the websites I visit, that you can call out for anything you desire, however aberrant or unlikely, and nearly always there comes an answer; it's a large world, we're never as solitary as we think, as unique or unprecedented, what we feel has always already been felt, again and again, without beginning or end.

He lay on me for some time, not moving or rather moving only to press me down, to ease out my pain and my will; he spread his length along mine, reaching until his hands were at my hands, coaxing free the fingers I had curled, and his feet found their place at my ankles, and then it was as if with his whole body he eased me, stretching and relaxing me at once. It was a delicious feeling, and again I admired his skill, how well he knew his instrument, how much I would take and how to bring me back from it. He was gentle, as he lay there he spoke to me, crooning almost, calling to me again *Kuchko*, the term of abuse that had become our endearment, *spokoino*, he said, relax, be calm. And I obeyed him, I could feel that fluid ache drain as he lay on top of me, moving just slightly, pressing me down and at the same time stretching me, pulling tenderly on each of my limbs, though soon his movement became something else. He had remained hard, though my own excitement had waned, had flowed out as the pain flowed in; and now it was his hardness I felt, he ground it into me, making my excitement return, not all at once but like an increasing pressure that provoked its own movement in response, a movement of my hips upward just slightly and back. It was a suggestion of movement, really, all that was permitted by his bulk on top of me, but it was enough to make him laugh again, that low, quiet, satisfied laugh I heard against my ear. *Iska li neshto*, he said, does she want something, and I did, I wanted something very much. He was moving more now, not just grinding but lifting his hips, which shifted his weight to his knees, which dug into the hollows of my own knees and pinned me more insistently down. He began to move more forcefully, rubbing the length of himself against me, and I could hear his breath quicken with the effort of it. Then he lifted himself more, and without moving his hands from my wrists he positioned his cock to fuck me, though he couldn't fuck me, I thought, he was dry and had done nothing to prepare me, with his hands or his mouth, and I felt myself tighten against him as he pressed forward, moving not violently but insistently. Wait, I said, speaking the word I had almost said before, wait, I'm not ready, but he said again *spokoino*, relax, be calm, he didn't try to enter me now but fell back to that insistent rubbing. He spoke softly as he rose again, crooningly, You're ready, he said, you want it, open to *gospodar*. *Ne*, I said, *ne*, wait, you need a condom, using the word *gumichka*, little rubber. He shifted his position at this, he released one of my wrists to wrap his arm around my neck, not choking me but taking hold of me, pressing the links of the chain into my skin. We don't need that, he said, I don't like them, he spoke close to my ear, intimately, persuasively, and it will hurt you more if I use one. He started to move again, pressing forward though I resisted him, you need a condom, I said, please, there's one in my pocket, let me get it, and I moved my free arm as if to lift myself up, setting it as a brace at my side. *Kuchko*, he repeated, not quite sternly but with disapproval, and then crooned again, don't you want to please me, don't you want to give me what I want? I did want to please him, and not only that, I wanted him inside me, I wanted to be fucked, but there was real danger, especially in this country; many people here are sick without knowing it, I knew, and knew too that he wouldn't be gentle, that I was likely to bleed, it's necessary, I said, please, I have one, we have to use it. Hush, he said again, *kuchko*, let me in, his voice quiet but his arm tightening around my neck, my throat in the crook of his elbow, let me in, and he pressed forward with real force. For a moment I wavered, I almost did let him in; it's what you wanted, I thought, it's what you said you wanted, I had asked him to make me nothing. But I didn't let him in, I said No, repeating it several times, my voice rising; no, I said, stop, *prestanete*, still using the polite form. Open, he said, but I didn't open, my whole body clenched in refusal, I did try to lift myself up now, but found I could hardly move at all. I was used to being the stronger one in such encounters, being so tall and so large, I was used to feeling the safety of strength, of knowing I could gather back up that personhood I had laid aside for an evening or an hour. But he was stronger than I was, and I was frightened as he held me down and pressed against me, shoving or thrusting himself. But he couldn't enter, I was clenched and dry and there was no forcing himself inside, and he grunted in frustration and said again Bitch, spitting the word, bitch, what are you to say no to me, and then he pulled back on my neck and bit my shoulder very hard, nearly breaking the skin, making a ring of bruises I would wear for days.

He lifted himself off me, shoving down so I lay flat again, and said loudly, almost shouting it, *Kakuv si ti*, what are you, *kakuv si ti*, and there was real anger in his voice now, not just frustration but rage, *kakuv si ti*, and then he grabbed a belt from the table, a leather strap, and brought it down hard on my back. The pain of it made me cry out, a womanish cry, and as he struck me he shouted *Pedal*, faggot, as if it were the answer to his question, *pedal, pedal*, each time striking me very hard as I cried out again and again, saying Stop, the single syllable, returning to my own language as if to air or waking, stop, I said in English, I'm sorry, stop. It wasn't just the beating that I wanted to stop but the whole encounter, the string of events I had set in motion, the will-lessness I had assumed, which had carried me now past anything I might want, and I said to myself what have I done, what have I done.

He did stop then, and in the sudden silence I could hear him breathing heavily, as I was, breathing or sobbing, I'm not sure which. I gathered myself to my hands and knees, moving slowly, it was the most I could manage; I was covered in sweat again, from exertion and from fear. It was over now, I thought, but then he spoke again, saying *Dolu*, down. I didn't contradict him but I didn't lie back down, I couldn't bear to return to the helplessness I had thought I wanted. *Dolu*, he said again, and when again I didn't obey him he lifted his foot and set it on my back, pressing as if to force me down. But I held firm, and so he reached down, not removing his foot, and grabbed the leash or chain where it hung, and as he straightened he pulled it tight, not with all his strength but enough that I felt it, and felt that he could choke me if he chose. He stepped off me then, moving behind me with the leash still in hand, and I tried to rise, lifting my chest both to slacken the chain and to rise to my feet, to stand for the first time in what seemed like hours. As I began to get up I must have shifted my knees apart, I must have moved in a way that opened myself to his foot, which struck me now hard between my legs, so it wasn't the chain that choked me but pain as I fell forward without a sound, unable to breathe, stripped clean of the will I had been gathering back in scraps; my arms collapsed and I fell forward and curled into myself in animal response. But he didn't let me curl into myself, he fell on top of me, he pushed or shifted me until I was available to him again, so that beneath pain and sharper than it I felt fear, a rising pitch of fear and protest and a terrible shame. He positioned himself as he had before, with his knees in my knees and his hands gripping my wrists, and in my confusion and pain I'm not sure if I struggled, or how much I struggled, though I did clench myself shut; he couldn't enter me at first, and again I heard him make that grunt or growl of frustration. But he was wet now, he must have spat into his palm and slicked himself with it, and when he lifted just slightly and brought himself down with his whole weight he did enter me, there was a great tearing pain and I cried out in a voice I had never heard before, a shrill sound that frightened me further, that wasn't my voice at all, and I choked it off as I twisted away from him, not thinking but in panic and pain, using all my strength. Maybe he was frightened too by my cry, maybe I had startled him; in any case I was free of him, I had thrown him or he had allowed himself to be thrown. He must have allowed it, I think, since he made no further attempt, though he could have done whatever he wanted; after my effort I lay exhausted, watching him where he lay on his back breathing hard.

Bitch, he said softly several times, softly but viciously, *mrusna kuchka*, dirty bitch, get out. It was a reprieve, permission to leave, and I pulled the chain from my neck and stood, after a fashion, hunched as I was around pain. I felt nothing of what I had thought I might feel in standing, I reclaimed nothing, nothing at all returned. I dressed as quickly as I could, though it seemed I was moving slowly, as if in a fog or a dream, I put my socks and my belt in my pockets, I left my shirt unbuttoned. I watched the man where he watched me, sitting now with his back to the wall. I turned away from him finally, I went to the door and felt something like panic again when the knob refused to turn. Like all doors here it had several locks and I looked at them hopelessly, turning first one and then another and finding the door still locked, more locked now that I had turned more latches, and this was like a dream also, of endlessness and the impossibility of escape; stupid, I thought, or maybe I whispered it to myself, stupid, stupid. The man rose then, I heard or felt him heave himself up and walk to the door. *Kuchko*, he said, not angrily now but mockingly, shaking his head a little, pacified perhaps by the fear that was evident as he reached around me to unlock the door, as I pressed myself as best I could into the wall behind me; there was nowhere to go, the corridor was narrow, and it was hard not to touch him as he opened the door, as I tried to slip past, feeling again what he wanted me to feel, I think, that if I left it was because he let me leave, that it was his will and not my own that opened the door. And then he seemed to change his mind, when I stepped into the dark hall he grabbed my shoulder, gripping me hard, not to pull me back but to spin me around, making me face him a final time. Things happened very fast then, I had brought my hands up when he grabbed me, to ward or fight him off, though I couldn't have fought him off, I've never struck anyone, really, never in earnest. Still, I lifted my hands, palms up at my chest, and when again as at the beginning of our encounter he spat into my face, which was why he had grabbed me and spun me around, to spit again with great violence into my face, I placed my hands on his chest and pushed or tried to push him away from me. But he didn't fall back, I hardly moved him at all, maybe he staggered just slightly but immediately he sprang forward, with the kind of savagery or abandon I could never allow myself he lunged to strike at me. Maybe he had staggered just slightly and that was why he missed, his aim failing as he lunged or fell forward into the hallway, where I was already moving toward the stairway, off-balance myself, almost reaching it before his hands were on me again, both of his hands now grabbing me and throwing me forward so that I fell down the stairs, or almost fell; by luck I stayed on my feet, though I landed on my right foot in a way that strained or tore something, I would limp for weeks. And maybe it's only in retrospect that I think I chose how I landed, though I have a memory, an instant of clearheadedness in which I knew he wasn't finished with me, though he was naked and it was dangerous for him I knew he would follow me, and so I think I decided as I fell forward not to catch myself against the concrete wall but instead to strike the small window there, hitting the pane with my right palm hard, shattering it. The noise did what I wanted, he turned and raced for his door, and in the instant I looked up at him I saw he was frightened. I ran or stumbled down the flights of stairs, and reached the door just as the hallway lights went on, some neighbor above drawn out by the sound.

It was very late, the boulevard was quiet, and if in a moment someone would emerge from the little convenience store (*denonoshtno*, its window said, day-and-night), if in a moment someone would emerge to investigate, I had time to get away, as I thought of it, walking one block and then another without passing a soul. I kept my head down, trying to be blank and unplaceable, trying to calm what I felt, which was pain and relief and shame and panic still, even though I thought I was clear, that I was far enough now to go on uncaught. But I couldn't calm what I felt, something rose in me I couldn't keep down, as I couldn't keep walking at the pace I had set; with each step my foot was more tender and there was something else, too, a nausea climbing to my throat, I was going to be sick. I turned quickly into the space between two buildings, an alleyway lined with trash bags and refuse, among which I bent over or crouched, unable to stand. But it wasn't with bile or sickness that I heaved but with tears, which came unexpected and fluent and hot, consuming in a way I hadn't known for a very long time, that maybe I had never known. I raised my hands, wanting to cover my face, though there was no one to see I was still ashamed of my tears, and I saw that my right hand was covered with blood. In the light from the street I could see where my wrist was torn, a small deep wound where it had caught on the glass. Stupid, I thought again, stupid, at the wound or my weeping, I'm not sure which. Why should I weep, I thought, at what, when I had brought it all upon myself, and I took one of my socks from my pocket and pressed it to the wound, wrapping it around my wrist and folding the cuff of my sleeve over it, not knowing what else to do.

It was a fit of weeping violent and brief, and as my breath steadied I felt a sense of resolution, that I had been lucky and must learn from that luck; I wouldn't go back to such a place, I thought, this would be the end of it. But how many times had I felt that I could change, I had felt it through all the long months with R., months that I had spent, for all my happiness, in a state of perpetual hunger; and so at the same time I felt it I felt too that my resolution was a lie, that it had always been a lie, that my real life was here, and I thought this even as I struggled to climb from the new depth I had been shown. And even as I climbed or sought to climb I knew that having been shown it I would come back to it, when the pain had faded and the fear, maybe not to this man but to others like him; I would desire it, though I didn't desire it now, and for a time I would resist my desire but only for a time. There was no lowest place, I thought, I would strike ground only to feel it give way gaping beneath me, and I felt with a new fear how little sense of myself I have, how there was no end to what I could want or to the punishment I would seek. For some moments I wrestled with these thoughts, and then I stood and turned back to the boulevard, composing as best I could my human face.

DECENT PEOPLE

But it isn't serious, he said, waving his hand at the snarl of traffic on the boulevard leading into the center, of course not, if it were serious we would be part of it, *nie shofyorite*, taxi drivers he meant, we would blockade the streets like we did during the Changes, everyone would be on strike. You could be proud in those days, he said, meaning 1989, when Communism fell, we were proud, we were organized. I was young then, it was a wonderful time. I could have left, he said, I could have gone anywhere, Europe, America, but I didn't want to go anywhere, I wanted to stay here. We thought it was the most exciting place to be, we thought we would make something out of our country, we had so much hope, do you understand, we felt so much hope because finally we were free. Free, he said, then sucked hard on his cigarette, turning to the window to blow the smoke away from me, we thought we would make something new but we didn't. It was the same assholes, he said—the word he used was *neshtastnitsi*, the literal meaning is something like unhappy or unlucky, the unfortunate ones—it was the same assholes who took over. It was still hot though it was the end of the afternoon, people were heading home from work, heading home or to the center, as we were, where already protesters were gathering as they had all week, in the hundreds and thousands. I had been watching them on the news but wanted to be among them in person, it felt like something remarkable was happening or about to happen in this country where so little happens, really, which is usually so quiescent. I wanted to see it for myself though it had nothing to do with me, of course, it wasn't my country, would never be my country, I was leaving at the end of the term. But it had been my home, as close to home as anywhere else, and I wanted the demonstrations to be more than a momentary spasm, I felt the hope that some of my students felt, my colleagues, I wanted it to be real. What does it matter which party takes over, he went on, *vse edno*, they're all the same, they're all thieves, look what they've done to my country. The traffic moved a little finally, he gripped the steering wheel again, the cigarette burned almost to the filter between the first and second fingers of his left hand. I could have gone away but I didn't, he said, *prostak*, idiot, I've fucked my life. He was still a young man, I thought, or at least he wasn't old, maybe a few years older than I was, too young to talk the way he was talking. Too young by American time, I mean, different times pertain in different places. He was dressed like a young man, too, in jeans and a worn T-shirt, his face rough with two or three days' stubble and glistening just slightly with sweat, as mine was, even with the windows open it was hot in the car. He glanced at me every now and again, his eyes not holding mine. *Vizh*, he said then, look, I understand them, it's impossible to live a normal life in Bulgaria, I mean if you want to follow the laws, pay your taxes, you can't survive here and be honest, only criminals survive. I don't mean you don't go to expensive restaurants or bars, you don't have a good time, I mean you can't put food on the table, you can't have a normal life. I want to live like that, do you understand, I want to live in a normal country. We had gotten past the Pliska Hotel finally, where all the buses stop, the traffic was heavy still but moving. So I understand the protesters, there need to be protests, this government needs to disappear—but there's nowhere to turn, the politicians, *vsichki sa pedali*, he said, they're all faggots. He hadn't asked me anything during the ride, none of the usual questions about who I was or where I was from, he couldn't be sure how much of what he said I understood. But it didn't matter, he was talking for his own benefit, I thought, for his own relief. We slowed again to a stop and he gave a low whistle as he looked at the traffic, which was completely jammed ahead near Levski Stadium, where the boulevard we were on crossed another by the little river that ran through Sofia, cordoned off in a concrete canal. It was called Perlovska, the pearly river, which made me laugh, since it was a drainage ditch, really, almost an open sewer; it was only called Perlovska on maps, nobody used the name in real life.

My girlfriend, the driver said, she yells at me all the time, she says I work too hard, she wants me to spend more time with her, you know, she doesn't understand. She's from the mountains, her parents still live in the village, she likes to go there on the weekends, she wants me to go too. But tell me, he said, how do I have the time to go, I work twelve, fifteen hours a day, every day, you understand, I never take a day off. I love the mountains, he said, as if defending himself, running his fingers through his hair, which was cut close to the skull, I would love to go to the mountains, to get out of Sofia, in the mountains it's clean, the air is good, you can breathe there, it's not like here. Sofia used to be clean, he said, when I was a kid, I hated the Communists but you have to be honest, they kept things clean, it wasn't like it is now. And people took care of each other then, he said, we were all fucked but we had solidarity. Now people just say fuck off—*maika ti*, he said, which means your mother, it's a kind of contraction, when people are really angry they say *maika ti da eba*, I fuck your mother—nobody cares about the others, everybody steals whatever they can. Do people take care of each other in America, he said then, the first question he had asked me though he didn't want an answer, he went on right away, I know they do, he said, I've never been to America but I have the idea that you care for each other there. We were still stopped in traffic, he shifted anxiously in his seat. That's good about the protests, maybe, he said, they show that people believe in solidarity, the young people, we've forgotten but to them it's still important. *Mozhe bi*, he said again, maybe, I don't know. He took his pack of cigarettes from a cupholder in the center console and knocked one into his palm. Well, he said, lighting it, buddy, *priyatelyu*, this traffic isn't going to move anytime soon. He suggested I get out and walk, that way he could take the next exit and head back to Mladost. We settled up then, I grabbed my backpack from between my legs and hooked my fingers through the latch of the door.

Blagodarya, I said, hesitating a moment before leaving the little intimacy his speech had made, and he held out his hand. *Uspeh*, he said as I took it, good luck, and then he released it to fiddle with the radio, dismissing me with a blast of American rock.

It was a bit of a walk to the gathering point, which was in front of the Archaeological Museum, on a stretch that featured the city's most impressive architecture, its public face: the huge cathedral, with its domes and bells, and state buildings, the university and National Assembly, august and classical. It was an architecture of aspiration, a new nation declaring its ideals. Much of the protesters' anger had converged here, at the Assembly especially, where there had been a dramatic moment in an earlier wave of protests, a couple of months before. It had been late, almost midnight, and the representatives were huddling inside, waiting for the protesters to leave, as they always did, once they had spent their anger in shouting. But something happened that evening, there was a shift, the anger didn't disperse but grew ominous, dense and pressured. With every representative who left the protesters had grown angrier, their insults more virulent, their chants more raucous, to the point that the politicians who remained were too frightened to leave, the police had to intervene, they brought in a bus to evacuate them. But the crowd wouldn't let them leave, they pressed themselves against the bus, began rocking it back and forth, and then there were balaclavaed men with bottles and metal pipes, and in a clip repeated again and again on the news one of them leapt up and struck one of the windows, shattering it. This escalation seemed to give the crowd pause, it was as if there were an indrawn breath, a hesitation that might have been the prelude to real violence except that it gave the line of police reinforcements a chance to break through, using their shields to push the protesters back, opening a path for the bus to escape.

Probably it had something to do with the weather, the fact that the most recent protests had remained peaceful; Sofia is wonderful in springtime, and even with the unseasonable heat it was a glorious spring. At Orlov Most the little vendor stalls were heaped with flowers and with cherries, swollen and voluptuously red; old women brought them from their villages, they were the most delicious cherries I had ever tasted. I bought some now from a round squat woman who called out *sladki, sladki*, promising they were sweet. She put great handfuls in a plastic sack, a bread bag turned inside out—I saw she had a whole heap of these sacks next to her in a garbage bag, she must have been collecting them all winter. The bag she handed me was half full, more than I wanted, she had filled it before I could tell her to stop. She was wearing a thin, formless housedress with a floral pattern, almost a nightgown, the kind of thing my own grandmother wore, and her hair was the same, too, cut short and curled; probably the resemblance was why I stopped, though her hair wasn't my grandmother's gray but dyed a bright shade of red I had only ever seen in the Balkans. She weighed the cherries on an old balance scale, as she did so trying to sell me her flowers, that was all she had on her table, cherries and country flowers, daisies and black-eyed Susans and Queen Anne's lace, laid out in piles and also in prebundled bouquets, one of which she held out to me. For your girlfriend, she said, go on, she will be so happy. I laughed, thanking her but not taking the flowers, and she shrugged, disappointed. But she smiled again when I handed her a bill for five leva, telling her to keep the change, and she insisted I take a single black-eyed Susan, which I did, I would feel awkward carrying it through the streets but it would have been rude to refuse. I thanked her and slipped into the stream of people walking along the boulevard. Nearly everyone was headed for the protests, they carried signs and noisemakers, one man swung a bullhorn at his waist. They were young people mostly, some of them with shaved heads or dyed hair, the various strands of Sofia's alternative scene, a kind of neo-hippie style of torn jeans and denim jackets; but really there were people of all kinds, men and women coming from the office, couples pushing bikes or strollers, one young man with his daughter on his shoulders, her ringlets of brown hair crowned with a chain of flowers. People were laughing, the mood wasn't angry at all, it was ebullient, and I slipped the stem of the black-eyed Susan through the buttons of my shirt, so that the bright head hung at my heart. That put me in mind of something, a flower for a heart, there was a line of a poem I almost remembered, something from O'Hara or Reverdy; I couldn't quite catch it but the feel of it made me smile. Police were in the street directing traffic, ushering the last cars through before they closed the boulevard for the march, but for now we stayed on the sidewalk, moving more slowly as it grew more crowded, which just increased our fellow feeling: people smiled to one another in a way that was unusual in Sofia, couples drew closer together, parents pulled their children near, keeping a hand on the top of their heads, on the nape of their necks. Bulgarian flags were everywhere, dangling from breast pockets or the straps of backpacks, one woman had four or five of them tucked into the long braid of her hair. Children waved them in the air, and some adults did, too, though we hadn't made it to the protest yet. Or maybe we had, we were the protest already, I guess, we had become a kind of parade. The cherries burst in my mouth, firm and ripe, sweet with a dark sweetness, gorgeous, like a low frequency. I spat the pits in my palm and dropped them a little guiltily into the gutter.

My phone buzzed with a text from D., telling me to meet him at the fountain in front of the Presidency. He was one of the first friends I had made in Bulgaria, a journalist and a poet, an alumnus of the school where I taught. We had met at some function where he was held up as an example, since after college and graduate school in the States he had decided to come back, as almost none of our students ever did; if you came back it meant you had failed, our students thought, but D. hadn't failed, it was an important example. The boulevard was blocked off after the intersection with Rakovski and we spilled out into the street, which was already full of people, as was the square in front of the Presidency. This had yellow police barricades in front of it but was otherwise protected only by the usual ornamental guard, two men in nineteenth-century uniforms staring blankly and unfazed, bayonets held stiffly at their sides. The police were gathered across the boulevard, in front of the former Communist Party headquarters, which served as Parliament offices now and where there was a much larger space kept free from protesters, the distance a bottle could be thrown, I thought—but they were relaxed, most of them held their helmets under their arms. Their riot shields were stacked in piles leaning against the bus they had traveled in on, the size of an American schoolbus, painted blue and white. They were smiling and talking with one another, with the protesters, toward whom they had expressed a benevolent neutrality, claiming in public statements that they were keeping the protests safe, that so long as they remained peaceful they had no intention of putting a stop to them; and the protesters reciprocated, one man stood now in front of them with a sign that read WE THANK OUR FRIENDS THE POLICE. The hope was that by saying it one could make it so, I thought, and so far the hope had held. Interspersed among the crowd were large white vans, teams of newscasters; cameramen stood on their roofs, next to the satellite dishes, scanning the crowd. People were milling about, many of them holding their signs above their heads to block the sun; it could have been a fair, almost, the crowd was bright with balloons, with spinning pinwheels children waved, with the sounds of whistles and handheld drums. Near the fountain, in the shade of a tree, a man had set out a table with these trinkets, most of all with the little Bulgarian flags that he held out to passersby, calling out *po levche sa*, one lev each. There were other street vendors, too; the air was sweet with roasted walnuts, and people were carrying little plastic bags of sunflower seeds, bottles of water still sweating with condensation.

I couldn't see D. at first, the area around the fountain was packed with people. Children ran around the fountain's edge, weaving past their parents, bumping into strangers, and playing in the water, too, though there were signs forbidding it; they shrieked, arms pressed tight to their sides, as the spray soaked their clothes. But then I noticed him, he had hoisted himself onto the base of a lamppost and was scanning the crowd. I waved and his face brightened when he saw me. He was a few years younger than I, with shaggy black hair that hung into his eyes if he let it go too long between haircuts, as he had now. He wasn't obviously beautiful but he was beautiful, it was a combination of charm and intelligence, a kind of earthy old-world grace, and of the wiry athleticism I felt when we hugged, a little awkwardly to spare the flower. You've been working out, I said when he pulled back, and he smiled, raising both his arms in a muscleman pose. It had taken me a while to be sure he was straight, he was so warm with his friends, he spoke a language of endearment, of casual caresses and kisses to the cheek and forehead, flirtation was his natural mode of congress with the world. This annoyed me sometimes in others, it could seem like a taunt, or a demand to be adored; but D.'s affection was genuine, a kind of blessing, it made you happy to be with him. He led me to the patch of shade he had claimed under the trees that grew near the wall of the Archaeological Museum, where he had been standing with two other people. One of these was his mother, whom I knew well, and I took the flower from my shirt and held it out to her, which made her laugh, she took it and then pulled me to her for a hug. I'm sure my face showed my surprise when D. introduced me to the older man standing with them; I had read his books, in Bulgarian and in English, he was the first writer I read when I decided years before to come to Sofia. *Za men e chest*, I said to him, shaking his hand, it's an honor, and he smiled, less at the sentiment, I thought, than at the formality of what I had said, which was so out of tune with the festive atmosphere, with his friendship with D., which was old and deep, with the shorts and sneakers he was wearing, I was suddenly a little embarrassed. Cherries, I said in English, I had almost forgotten their weight in my hand, and I held the bag out to him. He laughed, and as he reached his hand in the awkwardness was gone. D. took each of us by a shoulder, beaming, and said how happy he was for us to meet. I offered the cherries to him, too, telling him to take the bag, I had had enough. You brought us gifts, D. said, flowers and cherries, you brought us springtime, he said, which made everyone laugh.

The writer had already been saying his goodbyes when I arrived. He wouldn't march tonight, he said, he had come to watch the crowd gather but he had to get home to his daughter, it was her bedtime already. She would be getting cross, he said to me; he spoke the English of the British Institute, of the Cambridge exam. He was devoted to this girl, who was four or five; his Facebook page was full of pictures of her, of the two of them, he was a convert to fatherhood, having come to it late. She came the first couple of days, he said, but after that she refused, she wanted to stay home with her mother and read—she loves to read, he said, you've never seen a child who loves so much to read—she says the protests are boring. Smart girl, D. said, they *are* boring, every night is the same, it's not really a protest, it's just a boring party. He spoke as if he were picking up a conversation I had interrupted. They don't have any ideas, he said, throwing up his hands, what's the good of a movement without any ideas. No no, the writer said, please, you can't write that—D. was reporting on the protests for a newspaper in Britain, almost the first international coverage they would receive—please, that can't be your story. You have to say what the feeling is, the energy, but D. cut him off. The energy, he said, not sounding happy now, what the fuck is that? Look, if it's just energy, we should hope it stops, right away, energy without a plan can't build anything, it's more likely to make things worse. No, the writer said again, but he was already withdrawing, he put his hand on D.'s shoulder but it was a way of ending the conversation, not of drawing him near. I don't think you're right, he said, it's the future they want, you should do what you can to help them. He smiled then, he put his hand on D.'s face, cupping his cheek like a grandfather, a much older man. If you had children you'd see it differently, he said, switching to Bulgarian, you'd support them then. D. scoffed but the writer had already moved on, he reached his hand to D.'s mother, who took him by the arm instead. I'm going too, she said, I'll walk with you. D. kissed her cheek, and she thanked me again for the flower, which she held with her free hand as she and the writer set off for the metro stop a few blocks away, leaving D. and me alone. He looked at me and smiled, shrugging a little. He's a great writer, he said, but he's wrong about this. I didn't say anything; I wanted to take up the writer's side of things, but I knew I would lose the argument—I didn't have any arguments, really, just feelings, he would have laughed at them. And anyway the drums started beating then, and air horns blared, and there was a shift in the crowd, which grew still and then very slowly began to move. D. sighed. Okay, he said, I guess it's time, and he swung his backpack off his shoulder to take out a large camera, which he hung around his neck. It was his first time at the protests, too, he had followed them in the news but hadn't come out until tonight, to play the role of journalist, not citizen—he would wander around talking to people, he said, gathering material. There was another blast of horns, and D. invited me to join him. But I would have been in the way, and I wanted to be on my own for a bit, I told him I would find him later. The crowd was moving more decisively now, I stood for a while at the fountain and watched it pass. People held their signs at attention, not using them for shade anymore, and everywhere I saw the word OSTAVKA, resignation, the protesters' primary demand. A golden retriever twisted among the crowd, unleashed, his tail crazily wagging, until he paused in front of a young girl with Bulgarian flags painted on her cheeks, who patted him once or twice before he rushed off again.

I was there to join them, but something held me back. I stood scanning the crowd until I saw, among all the Bulgarian red and green and white, a little rainbow flag, then another, a whole group of five or six people waving them alongside their posterboard signs. I knew them, or most of them, they were activists I had met over the years, and I cut through the crowd toward them. S. greeted me first, tucking his posterboard under his arm to shake my hand. He was in his midtwenties, tall, with longish brown hair he frequently tossed out of his eyes, the gesture of an eighties pop star. He had come in from Varna, where he ran one of the only activist organizations I had heard of outside of Sofia. It had been in the news lately, they had tried to organize what he called an LGBT film festival, though it was really just a few chairs and a DVD player in a café. But even that was too much; on the second day a group of men barged in, they destroyed the television, they threatened anyone who came back. I mentioned this to him, saying it was terrible, outrageous, but he waved the words away. Those assholes, he said, it was just bullshit theater, the police were there the next day but they didn't come back. He was more upset about the Pride parade in Sofia, which had been canceled; when the city had expressed concern about security during the protests, the organizers had put out a statement that they were postponing the event as an act of solidarity, that it was a time for Sofians to stand together. *Obedineni sme*, they said, we're united as Bulgarians, which is total bullshit, S. said, what kind of message is that, it says we have to choose between being gay and being Bulgarian, fuck that, it's so fucking homophobic. He winced as an air horn blew nearby. And fuck the city, he said, they can't just decide not to protect us. If they want to be part of the EU they have to make it safe for us to march, it's bullshit to give them permission not to try. He gestured to the rest of the group. So we're doing Pride anyway, he said, they should know we're here, they shouldn't be able to ignore us. Even so, their posterboard signs were mostly discreet, one with the words NIE SME S VAS, we're with you, with rainbows in the corner, another with TOLERANTNOST in thick black letters against the white. Only two of them carried signs that were more demonstrative: S., whose sign read NIE PROTESTIRAME BEZ HOMOFOBIYA, we're protesting without homophobia, and K., a woman my age from Dobrich, a small city where she worked translating technical English but spent most of her time on message boards and chat rooms, often enough on the phone, counseling gay teenagers—she called them her children—sometimes talking to them through the night. This accounted for the harried look she always wore when I saw her, the dark circles under her eyes, the heaviness with which she moved. She was admirable, everything about her spoke of sacrifice, and something in me shied away from her, I didn't doubt the good she did but I avoided her whenever I could. S. had been one of her children, years before, and he remained devoted to her; I had heard him say that she had saved his life, that she inspired the work he did. She nodded when I walked up, but didn't offer to shake my hand. Hers was the largest sign, with the letters LGBT and beneath them I NIE SME BUL-GARI, we're Bulgarians too.

We moved slowly along Tsar Osvoboditel. We had already passed the university, where in the laps of the statues of the founding brothers, scholarly and distinguished in their chairs, protesters had placed identical OSTAVKA signs. Skaters sloped up and down metal ramps in the Knyazheska Garden, and behind them rose the monument to the Soviet army, at the top of which huge cast-iron soldiers raised their rifles to the sky. It was pure Communist kitsch but for all that impressive, especially with the light waning, the mountains a jagged dark ring at the horizon, it was one of my favorite views in Sofia. The chants were starting up in earnest, they began at the front of the march and traveled backward, almost antiphonal, the three syllables of *ostavka* moving up and down the line. There was an angrier chant aimed at the socialists, *cherveni boklutsi*, red trash—there was a coalition government but the socialists had taken the brunt of the protesters' anger, as they usually did; they weren't really socialists at all, I'd heard people say, they were just the Communist Party rebranded. But each time this chant rose up it died down quickly, it couldn't get any traction. S. told me that his sign was inspired by this chant, which sometimes became *cherveni pedali*, red faggots, among the angrier groups of protesters, he had heard it almost every night he had marched. But the mood now wasn't angry at all, people passed bottles of wine and beer over the heads of children. I said goodbye to S. and the others, wishing them luck, and drifted among the crowd, which was easy to do, little groups of friends hung together but otherwise there was plenty of space between marchers. The protests were organized online, on Facebook and Twitter, and many of the signs were marked with hashtags, #ostavka and #mirenprotest, peaceful protest, giving me the eerie sense of being on- and offline at once. JOURNALISTS! one sign read in English, TELL THE WORLD WHAT'S HAPPENING HERE. A sense of bewilderment and grievance had grown as the days passed; how is this not news, my students asked me, why doesn't anyone care, and I was at a loss to answer them, except that it was the season of uprisings, of the Arab Spring and Taksim Square, protests that were larger and more violent. There was only so much attention to go around, I supposed, it ran out before it could reach Bulgaria.

At Orlov Most, the protesters turned onto the boulevard that runs alongside the canal. This left much of the bridge free, and protesters had set up a little carnival there, coloring with chalk on the pavement, painting flags on children's cheeks. At the far end of the bridge a man with a tuba played a jaunty bass line as another man, in a T-shirt and jeans and an NYC baseball cap, chanted or sang; I couldn't quite catch the words, but whatever they were they made the people gathered around him laugh and cheer. I paused to watch them, leaning against the rail of the bridge (the Perlovska passed a couple of meters below, a muddy stream), when I felt a hand tentative on my shoulder. I startled a little, I had been lost in my thoughts, and M. smiled at me apologetically when I turned. But I was happy to see her, I surprised myself by greeting her with a hug, though I almost never hugged my students; I could see that she was surprised too, surprised and pleased, she was smiling when I pulled away. She was a senior, a short, lovely girl with auburn hair that hung in curls around her cheeks, a serious student, though she didn't care much for literature; her heart was in science, she said, in the laboratory, in arcane things I couldn't begin to understand and that she would study next year in Berlin. *Gospodine*, she said to me now, isn't this amazing, and she made a gesture that took in everything, the marchers, the tuba, the gray of the bridge, the slow trudge of the Perlovksa, it's so good that you're here. The crowd of protesters flowing past the end of the bridge had thinned, and as we approached them to join the march again M. pointed down the stretch of Tsar Osvoboditel we had walked up, where now three figures with push brooms were gathering litter into large plastic bags, which they piled at each corner for pickup. Can you believe it, she said, they're making sure the city doesn't have anything to complain about, have you ever seen the streets so clean? It's so inspiring, what they're doing, she said. We joined the march again, which was quieter here in the back; most of the shouting was ahead of us, the drums at the front of the crowd were a distant sound. The tuba on the bridge blurted a few last notes, then stopped. I've come here every day, M. said, walking beside me, it makes me so happy to be here. Some people walking nearby began shouting *Ostavka*, picking up a chant that had migrated from the front of the march, and M. joined them for a few rounds, looking at me a little sheepishly. I didn't join in, I hadn't joined in any of the chants, even though I felt moved to; it wasn't my country, I kept saying to myself, it wasn't my place, but I was sorry when M. fell silent too. We walked a little faster, moving back into the middle of the boulevard, headed toward NDK, the Palace of Culture. One side of the street was lined with apartment buildings, the gray of their façades broken by large flags draped from the balconies, on almost all of which people stood watching, elderly men and women, many of them waving, as if to say they would be with us if they could. On the other side of us the trees lining the canal were catching the last of the light, the new leaves incandescent, Sofia was more beautiful to me then than I had ever seen it.

There's never been anything like this, M. said then, I mean maybe in 1989 but nothing I've ever seen. Something's really happening, I feel like I'm part of something, not just here but something bigger. It's the same as what's happening in Taksim Square, in Brazil, the Arab Spring, something is happening, something real, I think there's a chance for things really to change. I felt this too, it wasn't to challenge her that I asked what she thought that change would be. She shrugged. I'm not sure, she said, but I feel like we'll figure it out. She paused. I feel powerful in a way I never have before, she said, and then she glanced at me and laughed, I feel like one of the *opalchentsi* on Shipka. These were Bulgarian volunteers who fought with the Russians against the Ottomans, there was a poem about them by Ivan Vazov that every Bulgarian knew; I had heard a poet declaim it once, drunk at a dinner party, the room quiet with reverence. I feel the power of the people, she said gingerly, cringing at the cliché. Then she laughed again, pointing, and I saw that ahead of us a group of women were dancing on the sidewalk, their hair wet, their sundresses clinging to their bodies, and several stories above them an elderly man, shirtless and bald, his skin hanging loose around his frame, held a garden hose, pointing it up and half blocking the end with his thumb so that water fell down like rain. It was his gift to us, a chance to cool down, though most of the marchers avoided it, leaving it to the young women, who would be cold soon enough; the heat was fading, even on warm days the nights could be cool. It was an instant allegory, youth and age, Hephaestus and the Graces. And then my mind shuffled to the side a step and I thought of the water cannons in Taksim Square, of the luck that had held here so far. M. turned her head as we passed them, then looked back at me, smiling. My parents don't like that I come, she said, they don't like the government but they're afraid of violence, they're afraid I'll get in trouble with the police. But it's not like that at all, she said, people aren't angry, there's so much joy here, she said, they don't understand that, have you ever seen so much joy? It makes me wish I weren't leaving, she went on, my whole life I've been dying to get out of here and now I feel like I want to stay. This made me remember the taxi driver and what he had said about the Changes, how he had wasted his life for an idealism that had curdled, but I didn't say this, I put my arm around her and squeezed her shoulder, another breach of decorum. I mean, look at that, she said after I dropped my arm, and she pointed at a sign being carried by a man just in front of us. The crowd had bunched and slowed as people climbed the stairs that led from the boulevard up to the plaza at NDK. I almost never came to NDK this way, I always circled around to the other side. I only climbed these stairs once a year, I realized, for the Pride march, when the organizers used the stairs for a security check; we opened our bags and showed our IDs and had colored plastic bands attached to our wrists, so that the police could tell us apart from the protesters who would line our path. M. was pointing at a poster that showed a bearded man's face, and beneath it in block letters the name Vazov, the writer who had given M. her *opalchentsi*, and beside that another face, this one labeled Botev, another beloved poet. There was a whole group of them marching together, each with the face of a writer: there were Elin Pelin and Petko Slaveykov, and my favorite of the classic writers, Yordan Yovkov, the most elegant, he should be better known in English. Isn't that beautiful, M. said, tell me, where else do they march with their poets, and I had to admit that I didn't know, certainly not in America, I said, that's something you would never see there, and she smiled, I could see this gratified her.

We had talked about those writers in one of my classes earlier that week. It was a conversation class, which the Ministry required though it was useless for our students, who were fluent and spoke English all day; we only met for an hour once a week, but it was a struggle to fill the time. I had asked a few of them to choose a short video, anything they wanted, something they could talk about and get the class talking too. We had just watched something about Bulgaria, a promotional clip from the tourism board, which had sweeping aerial shots of mountains and countryside, of fields of sunflower and lavender, and then curious historical reenactments, men in medieval armor riding on horseback, women in nineteenth-century folk dress dancing the horo, all of it to a soundtrack of bagpipes and drums. It makes me feel proud, the student who brought it in said, there are so many problems in Bulgaria, but this, I don't know, it makes me feel proud for my country. She sat down then, quickly, relieved—she wasn't in my regular English class, I taught her that single period and didn't know her well, and she was quiet, one of the students I had to encourage to speak. She had barely settled in her chair when another student started talking, a girl I knew well and whom I never had to encourage; it was the opposite with her, I had to rein her in at times, which was my only job in that class, to hold the reins, not to steer them in any particular direction but to try to equalize engagement. This student was bursting to speak, it was all she could do not to interrupt. I'm sorry, she said, I'm sorry, I don't mean to diss your video—her English was the best in the class, she was a hair's breadth from sounding like any American kid—I don't mean to diss your video, but I'm so sick of this nostalgia bullshit. Sorry, she said, glancing at me, though she knew I didn't care if they cursed in class, sorry, but all this men-on-horseback crap, what does that have to do with Bulgaria, I mean with Bulgaria now. The hair's breadth made a difference; there's a kind of uncanny valley in language, competency can overshoot the mark, so that however perfectly we speak a foreign language speaking it too casually feels like imposture, I don't know why. I like horses, a boy interjected, getting a laugh, and she rolled her eyes. No, really, she said, this is the problem, when we want to be proud we think of the *natsionalno vuzrazhdane*, or we think of *Bulgariya na tri moreta*, we think of Tsarevets. She was right, I thought, though I didn't say anything; they were at the core of what my students thought of as their national identity, the nineteenth-century liberation and Bulgaria's medieval greatness, when its borders had touched three seas, *tri moreta*, a phrase the far right used to stoke nationalist feeling and that adorned tourist T-shirts at every cheap souvenir shop. But that doesn't say anything about how we live now, she said, it's all just Kill the Ottomans, it doesn't tell us anything about what it means to be Bulgarian now. The temperature rose a little at this; some of the students leaned forward in their seats, which were situated around a group of desks we had pushed together to make a kind of conference table, I wanted them to look at each other as they spoke. What does, then, a boy asked, what do you think does tell us about Bulgaria now, and another boy said Berbatov, the soccer star, which made half of the class laugh and the other half groan. Nothing, my student said, raising her voice, nothing does, that's our problem, that's why the protests won't go anywhere, we have no idea how to be Bulgarian in the real world, we have no idea how we should be. The temperature rose still further at this, a number of voices spoke at once, making noises of protest or skepticism, come on, I heard, and *gluposti*, nonsense, and then my student started to speak again in defense. I had let the reins go too slack, though I wanted to watch things play out the conversation was too hot, a couple of students were looking my way, I needed to intervene.

Poetry! I exclaimed, sitting up straight in my chair, which had the effect I wanted; they all turned to me, silent, less obedient than bewildered. I looked at them a moment, a kind of caesura, and then I repeated it, Poetry, as though it were the obvious answer to a question, the answer they already knew. That's what poets can do, I said, poets and artists; they give us ideas to buy into, for whole countries to buy into. Like Whitman, I said, whom they had all studied, he was part of the tenth-grade curriculum; my own tenth-graders were reading him now, *Song of Myself*, and I found it was a different poem because of the protests, which became the context for our reading, though I had read it dozens of times I read it differently now. Think of what he wants to do in that poem, I said, and when the country was at war with itself, absolutely broken; he wants to make an image of America anyone can buy into. Like that miraculous section, and I used that word, miraculous, I was getting excited, I was getting swept up in Whitman as I always did, it was what I loved about him and what I mistrusted, too, the feelings he could arouse that could swamp judgment. That section where all he does is name things, I said, well, not things, people, it's just a list, he wants it to include everyone, he wants to find a place for everyone. An equal place, I went on, though I was talking too much now, and a place in his affection, too. There are those wonderful moments he puts in parentheses, like a whisper, do you remember, where he tells us he loves the person he's just named. That's what he thought democracy was, I said, a poem that named things and made an occasion for you to love them; he wanted to stitch America up, I said, he wanted to break all the divisions down. There's only one time he does the opposite, it's in that same list, where he puts a prostitute right next to the president, do you remember? None of them did, but they were paying attention, less interested maybe in the poem or what I was saying than in my excitement, which they observed like some freakish natural phenomenon, I thought. There's a crowd making fun of the prostitute, I said, and that's the one time Whitman separates himself, he says they laugh at you, but I do not laugh at you. And that's the problem, I hurried on, that's the problem with democracy, the danger of crowds, it's the problem with the protests, too: how do you take a crowd and turn it into a populace, how do you take the voice of a crowd and turn it into the vox populi, the voice of a people. I glanced at the clock and saw that class was almost over, the bell would ring soon. People have to come together without losing their ability to think, Whitman calls it a "thoughtful merge," the whole idea of democracy depends on it. And look, I don't think a poem can do what he thought it could. He wanted his poem to *be* America, like magic, he wanted his poem to fix everything that was wrong with the country. Which was a lot! I said, trying to lighten the tone, which still is a lot, but what he did was to make an image of America that still feels like something I want to buy into, it still feels like the best image of ourselves. I stopped then, not knowing how to go on, and I was grateful when the bell rang, it let me raise my voice and say So go be poets, which released them from my overheated feeling and gave them permission to laugh.

The sun had fully set now, and between the streetlamps in the park at NDK there was utter darkness. We passed the entrance to the underground passageway, where there was a metro stop now, still new, and also the toilets where men went for sex, where I had spent so many weekend evenings;

walking with my student I felt the weird dissonance of my private and public lives. M. had been walking quietly, listening to the sound of the drums that drifted back to us from the front of the march. People weren't shouting as we walked through the park at NDK, the mood was restrained, contemplative, a little respite from the noise. Some people had let their signs drop in the dark, tucking them under their arms, but others still held them aloft, and I saw that several people were wearing glow bracelets, little rings of light that hovered over their heads. I asked M. if she usually came with friends, if there were many students marching from the school. Not so many, she said, and not my friends, usually I come alone. Lots of parents are scared, she said, and anyway we have so much work for school, it's hard to have time for anything else. But this is important, she went on, it's important for my country, it's important that the young people are here. I don't know, she said, some of my friends say it's stupid to come because we're leaving so soon, but I don't feel like that, it's still my country, she said, even if I'm leaving. Maybe I'll come back if things get better, I would like to come back. That's the real problem, I said, agreeing with her, so many people leave, so many of the best people, it's hard for things to get better when so many people leave. We had crossed onto Vitosha now, where there was more light, I could see her face when she turned to look at me. Do you think we're wrong to leave, she asked me, do you think we should stay? I hesitated before answering. It wasn't my place to answer, of course, and I told her this, and also I had left my own country, where there were so many problems, where I had done so little, really, to stand against them. But no, I said finally, I don't think you're wrong. You only have one life, I said, and I want you to be happy, I want you to go where you can live most fully, and even as I spoke I could hear the argument against each of my phrases canceling out what I said, I didn't know what I thought. But you're going back, M. said, you must be excited about that, to be going home. I'm not going home, I said, what would that even mean, I'm going back to America but I'm not going home. And maybe I won't stay, I said, I don't know, I like living abroad. And then I threw up my hands, I don't know anything, I said, don't listen to anything I say.

Part of Vitosha was a pedestrian zone, and the restaurants and cafés that lined it had seating that spilled out onto the street, some with tables laid out in elegant white, others with low couches for sprawling with cigarettes or water pipes. I was surprised that these were full, the protests hadn't put a dent in the crowds out to enjoy the evening. There were the usual tourists for whom the parade was a spectacle, they pointed their cameras at us, but also Bulgarians, some of whom sat with their backs resolutely turned, determined to ignore the chants of *ostavka* and the more aggressive chants of *cherveni boklutsi*, red trash, which had increased with the darkness, as had the presence of men wearing Guy Fawkes masks. There weren't many of them but they added a different note to things, a note of incivility, a discordant note, I thought, which was amplified by the fact that there weren't as many children now; it was a long march, they must have gotten tired. There were more police at the Palace of Justice, wearing their riot gear now but still relaxed; they were chatting among themselves with their visors lifted, shields propped on the ground. A couple of them were sitting on the stairs leading up to the palace, a young man leaned back against one of the stone lions there. D. had once pointed out to me that on one of these lions the legs are in the wrong position, the fore and hind legs of the same side stretch away from each other; it's supposed to suggest the cat in motion but no animal walks like that, D. said, if it walked like that it would fall over. It's the perfect symbol, he said, laughing, the Bulgarian lion. You know it's the word we use for our money, *lev*, as if our money has ever been a lion! A kitten, maybe, he said, the runt of the litter, and this made him laugh again.

Just past the palace we turned onto a side street I didn't know, which narrowed as it moved away from the boulevard, making the march slow down and bunch up. At the same time the noise grew louder, the drums in the darkness ahead of us started striking in unison in series of six beats, the rhythm of *cherveni boklutsi*, the syllables spaced out, each given equal weight, and there was the clamor too of air horns sounding all at once, a terrible sound, which lasted a minute or two and then died away, the drums receding also. A couple of blocks ahead the march had turned another corner, and this created a kind of bottleneck, slowing everything down further. The street was poorly lit, we were in darkness again, and now there were more police; they lined one side of the street, with their helmets on and their plastic shields raised. What's going on, I asked M., and she told me that we were approaching the headquarters of the Socialist Party, that every night the march took that route. There was another battery of air horns ahead of us, not as loud as the first but loud enough, the sound reverberated in the little street. It was an old street, with elegant, turn-of-the-century houses and even older dwellings, squat and unadorned, which had escaped the bombs of World War II and the building initiatives of the Communists and now were on the point of collapse. We were packed together now, barely moving though I still felt the impulse to move, the impulse of the crowd behind me. We were penned in, almost brushing shoulders with the people beside us, and I felt M. draw closer to me.

We inched forward, and then the noise began again just in front of us, and everyone around me started shouting as they turned to face a long building of concrete and glass, five or six stories high. Only the sculpture in front of it marked it out, I had passed it before without paying much attention to the building it adorned. It showed seven or eight figures in battle, some taking aim with rifles, others cradling fallen comrades, the whole dominated by a large, stylized figure of a woman on one knee, her arm flung forward, the fingers outstretched in a gesture that had always seemed moving to me, more moving now that she was outlined by the single lit window of a convenience store behind her. The march had come to a standstill, people were yelling *cherveni boklutsi* again and again as they shook their fists, suddenly a man standing right beside me sounded his air horn. Jesus, I must have said, covering my ear and shaking my head a little like an animal, and M. looked up at me, concerned. The mood was changing as the chant broke down and became something less choate and more animalistic, hisses and boos, and then I felt the pressure to move again, not in the same direction as before but toward the building and the line of police guarding it. The police felt it too, that pressure, they came to attention, lifting their shields an inch or two and locking them in place.

I said something then, This could be bad or something to that effect, and I felt M.'s hand on my arm, though she couldn't have heard what I said, there was too much noise and anyway I had whispered it, I was saying it mostly to myself. Points of red light were tracing patterns on the building's concrete façade, people had brought laser pointers, which were harmless of course and also sinister, they aimed them like the laser sights of rifles. The sound of the crowd grew louder, that inchoate sound, formless and primal, inhuman, hardly animal now but primordial, chthonic, like a sound the earth would make. It wasn't an animal sound but it elicited an animal response, or did for me, anyway, a fear that would have made me run had there been anywhere to run to, that instead made me grow very still. At the front of the crowd now, facing the police, six or seven men in Guy Fawkes masks had suddenly appeared. The masks seemed like an invitation to violence, to commit it or be subjected to it, and I thought I could see the police they were facing lean forward as if to meet them. There was the sound of glass breaking, a bottle thrown over the heads of the police, and almost at the same time a weird crackling and sudden fluorescence of flat red light. Someone behind us had lit a flare, and in response the noise died down, as if everyone had taken a breath. But the pressure I had felt didn't dissipate, in the suspension of our breath it mounted and became unbearable, demanding release, and though we didn't quite move it was as if everyone leaned very slightly forward, a wave on the brink of cresting. We hung fire, that's what it felt like, that phrase from nineteenth-century novels I had never quite understood, I understood it now. Whatever happened I would be swept along with it, whether I wanted to be or not, what I wanted was irrelevant. In the light of the flare I saw a policewoman's face, a young woman, hardly older than M.; behind the plastic visor her eyes flicked from right to left in fear. And then, just as I felt myself lean further forward, propelled not by any will of my own but by a larger will, ready to spring, from the very back of the crowd a man began to sing. Immediately other voices joined him, soon everyone was singing the national anthem, which is restrained and minor-key, as much mournful as celebratory, nothing like my own country's anthem, and it was as if the crowd relaxed into it; the pressure that had built dissolved, the song caught it and dispersed it. The police relaxed too, leaning back again, the crowd began to move, the fear I had felt became relief and then, as we turned the corner, something like joy, which I saw reflected on M.'s face and on the other faces around me; everyone was smiling again, beneficent, a nation again, that was what I felt, an ideal nation.

People kept singing for a block or two as we left the Party headquarters behind, turning right on the narrow street just past it, they cycled through two or three verses before the song faded away once we reached Stamboliyski Boulevard. We had returned to civilization, I thought, we were passing shops and restaurants, their lit interiors calling us back from what we had almost become, it was unimaginable now. At the intersection with Vitosha, the beautiful old church, Sveta Nedelya, sat brooding in the pool of its lights. *Ostavka*, people were still chanting, but it felt half-hearted now, a matter almost of form. That hasn't happened before, M. said, meaning the moment at the Party headquarters, I was scared almost, she said, were you, and I admitted that I was, that for a minute I had thought things might get bad. But it's good that we're scared, she said. If we're scared, that means they're scared, too. She looked at me, her face bright in a streetlamp, then looked away. They need to be scared, she said, maybe that's the whole point, they need to know they should be scared of us.

We turned back onto Vitosha, where M. stopped and said goodbye, she would take the metro home. I guess I should do my homework, she said, squeezing my arm in farewell before deciding instead to give me a quick hug. I'm so happy I saw you, she said, it was so great to do this, and then she was gone. Other people were leaving too, streaming down into the metro or dispersing on foot, the march was thinning out. Those of us who stayed turned onto Tsar Osvoboditel again, beginning the last leg of the protest, bringing us back full circle. There were still people yelling *cherveni boklutsi* but not many, most people were walking quietly, chatting among themselves. I would follow the march to the end, I had booked a hotel room for the night, in the luxury hotel near the statue of the tsar; after the embassy warnings travelers were staying in hotels far from the protests, the rooms were cheap enough for me to afford. I would spend the night there and take the metro to campus in the morning. I glanced at my phone and saw that D. was already waiting for me to join him for a drink at the bar. He was right, D. had texted, meaning the writer I had met and the argument they had had, what's happening is better than I thought, I can't wait to talk to you, hurry up. We were still a few blocks away but a new chant had started up, *utre pak*, tomorrow again, it gave people fresh energy, everyone was chanting it, pumping their fists in the air. Even I joined in, *utre pak*, I wanted to see what it was like to chant with the others, but soon I felt foolish and stopped.

There are grassy areas along that part of the boulevard, little gardens set back from the lights of the street, and so I didn't see S. and his friends at first, they were gathered some distance from the pavement. A woman was standing and waving her arms above her head, that was what caught my attention, and as I approached I saw that S. was sitting on the ground, leaning into K., who had both her arms around him, and that he was holding something to his face. They had piled their signs in the grass beside them, what was left of their signs, they had all been torn to pieces. What happened, I asked the woman who had waved me over, and she answered in English, Some assholes showed up, she said, some of those assholes in masks, they grabbed our signs from us, and they hit S., she went on, when he tried to stop them they knocked him down. All these police and none of them did anything, she said, they're assholes too, when we went to find them they said they would send someone but that was twenty minutes ago. They don't care what happened to us, we've been calling them but they just keep telling us to wait. She motioned to a man standing to one side, who was gesturing with his free hand while he spoke quickly into his phone. I'm so sorry, I said, do you need anything, is there anything I can do, but she shrugged this away. Does S. need a doctor, I asked, should we take him, but he cut me off, *Ne*, he said loudly, not moving or lowering his hand from his eye, he was pressing a bag of ice to it, I saw now, and the woman shrugged again. The cowards, the woman said, they were here and then they were gone, in their stupid masks. And what they said to us, they told us we were spreading trash, there are children here, they said, they said we were being—and she paused, looking at the others as she said *bezsramni*, shameless. Indecent, K. said then, they said we were indecent, they called us dirty queers. She spoke quietly, despite the noise of the protests, she spoke without anger or any trace of emotion; I could see why her children found her such a comfort.

They're fucking liars, S. said, pulling away from K. to sit upright, though she kept one arm around him. He lowered the bag from his eye, but in the dark I couldn't see how bad it was, whether he was really hurt. *Obedineni sme*, he said, quoting one of their slogans, but we're not united, they don't want to be united with us. It's all the same, he said, all this work and it's always the same. No, K. said in her calm voice, no, that's not true, you know that's not true, but he snapped at her, he pulled away and said angrily It is true, it is true. He had been sitting with his legs stretched out but now he pulled his knees to his chest and wrapped his arms around them. I'm so stupid, he said, I thought it would be different here, I thought these were the good people, the better people, they say they hate the Nazis from Ataka but they're all the same, to us they're all the same, they hate us, he said, speaking more loudly now, they hate us, I don't understand it but they'll always hate us. I hate them too, he said, they'll never change, I hate this fucking country. *Mrazya vi*, he said then, louder still, I hate you. He was speaking to the protesters now, the last of them passing by on the boulevard, *mrazya vi, mrazya vi*, each time saying it more loudly and angrily, so that people began to look our way; it made me nervous, and the others too, everyone moved just slightly toward one another. But none of the marchers stopped, they looked at us a moment and then looked away. K. kept putting her hand on S.'s back and he kept shaking it off, he didn't want to be comforted. *Mrazya vi*, he said a final time, almost shouting it, and then his voice caught, he lowered his forehead against his knees. He let K. put her arm around him then, and after a moment he leaned back into her and returned the ice to his eye.

I looked at the others, who were sitting on the grass in silence, the woman who had called me over, the man with his phone lowered now, not pressed to his ear, whatever conversation he had been having was over; all of them seemed as helpless as I felt, they all kept their distance from S. Only K. was any use, she was holding him with both her arms again, rocking back and forth a little and murmuring to him in Bulgarian. The protesters had passed and the street was quiet, but I couldn't make out what she was telling him; whatever she was saying was having an effect, S. was calmer now. Finally the man with the telephone spoke, They're coming, he said, meaning the police, they say we should wait for them, they'll be here soon. That's what they said twenty minutes ago, someone said, and the man shrugged and then sat down, leaving me the only one on my feet. I felt my phone buzz in my pocket, D. again, probably wondering where I was, but I ignored it, I looked at S. and K. huddled together, and then at the street. Volunteers were cleaning up after the last protesters, a man and a woman, each with a broom and dust pail, each sweeping one side of the boulevard, collecting plastic bottles and bits of paper where they had gathered at the curb, the occasional discarded flag; and when their bins were full they carried them to a second woman who stood between them, holding a large garbage bag open. I wondered if they were the same people I had seen before, whether their entire protest consisted of cleaning up, that gesture M. had been so proud of, leaving the city better than they had found it, leaving it pristine. My phone buzzed again, but I didn't want to meet D. now, I would write him soon to say I wasn't coming, or not for a while. It was pointless for me to stick around, I couldn't do anything to help, I wasn't any help at all, but I let my bag drop to the grass anyway, I sat down with them to wait.

II

LOVING R.

CLEANNESS

I was at our usual table, next to the window that made up most of the restaurant's east-facing wall. We liked to look out on the garden, where even in mid-October there would usually have been diners talking and smoking at the tables that were empty now, stripped of their umbrellas and chairs, black metal chains locked around their legs. It was a lovely garden, its shrubs and flowers rare in Mladost, a green relief among the concrete desolation of so much of the neighborhood. There was nothing to be done about the sound of traffic nearby, or the exhaust that tainted the air, and of course one only had to look up to see the gray of the apartment blocks, which put an end to all greenness. We enjoyed it best from inside, we had learned, it was a place to rest our eyes. But tonight everything outside was movement and agitation, as it had been all week, ever since a great wind had swept into or descended upon or laid siege to the city, it's hard to know how to put it, or my sense of it shifted with the days. It came up from Africa, the guards at my school said, old men who greeted it with resignation; it carries sand from Africa, you'll feel it, it is a horrible wind. And they were right, there was something almost malevolent about it, as if it were an intelligence, or at least an intention, carrying off whatever wasn't secure, worrying every loose edge. It made the city's cheap construction seem cheaper, more provisional and tenuous, a temporary arrangement—as is true of all places, I know, though it's a truth I'd rather not acknowledge, of course I came to hate the wind.

R. was late, as always, and after half an hour I had begun to wonder whether he would come at all. He often canceled our plans, usually after I had rearranged my own schedule to accommodate his, however inconvenient it was; and sometimes he didn't give any notice, just an apology hours after I had given up waiting. It was a popular restaurant, busy with the dinner rush, and I could feel myself becoming a spectacle, quiet in a convivial room, a bit of negative space. I had already fended off several approaches from the servers, saying I was waiting for a friend, he was on his way, gesturing to my lifeless phone as though I had heard from him, though in fact he hadn't responded to the texts I sent. The waiters had become more insistent as the tables around me filled; soon I would have to order something or leave. Even inside we could hear the wind; it was a sound above our human voices, a sound beyond the scale of living things. I always forgave R. when he didn't appear, I accepted any excuse he offered, whatever my annoyance I never complained. I wanted to think of this as patience, but really I knew it was fear; I would push him away if I demanded too much.

I had been sitting too long now, I was steeling myself to

go, when with a sudden increase of noise and a change of pressure, a slight disorder in the air, the door opened and R. came in. He was wearing a hat and scarf and a heavy winter coat, though it wasn't very cold; but then he was from a warm country, it was his first real fall. He grew up in the Azores, and though his town seemed beautiful in the photos I had found online, orderly white houses brilliant against the sea, he would never go back there, he said; it was a small place, he hated small places. He saw me right away, and without waiting to be greeted by a server he began making his way over, pulling off his hat and scarf as he walked. I was struck again by his beauty, which was offhand and accidental, with his disheveled hair and ruffled clothes, a beauty stripped of self-regard. Even though it was familiar to me I felt it as a kind of physical force, not welcoming me but pushing me off, so that I was always astonished to find I could take him in my arms. This was what I did now, embracing him though I had intended to remain seated, to greet him coolly and punish him a little. We parted after a second or two, but not before I heard R. make a sound I had come to love, a little grunt of happiness, a homecoming sound, and all my irritation drained away.

It's crazy outside, he said as he sat down, gesturing to the window beside us, it's totally crazy, I've never seen anything like it, have you—but he went on before I could answer. He was sorry he was late, he said, he was supposed to go to a party but had bowed out at the last minute, and then it had been hard to persuade his roommate to go on without him. I thought I wouldn't be able to come, R. said, and I made a noncommittal sound, feeling my annoyance return. Oh, he

said, are you mad, and he wore an expression of such open-
ness and willingness to be in the wrong that it was impossible
to stay angry. I told him it was all right, that he shouldn't
worry, it was nothing. No, he said, it isn't nothing, I hate that
I can't see you when I want to, and he made a small gesture
with his hand, extending it slightly toward mine. We couldn't
touch, of course, it would be imprudent, but he flexed his
fingers in a way that I knew meant desire, that though he was
touching the polished wood it was me he wanted to touch.
This was clear in his expression, too, when I looked at his
face and he said very softly, almost mouthing it, *Skupi*, one of
the few words of Bulgarian he had learned. It means dear or
of great price, which was what I had thought on our second
or third meeting as he lay naked beside me and I ran my hand
along his side. I had said the word almost without intending
to, *Skupi*, and he asked me what it meant and then drew me
to him and whispered it like an affirmation in my ear. It had
become our private name for each other, and I think it was
then, when we first uttered the word, that I realized I was
caught by him, that however things turned out they would
have consequence, and I was both frightened by this and
gave myself over to it, I decided I would let whatever might
happen between us happen.

I remembered this when he spoke the word, and then, as if
dispelling the atmosphere he had created, he turned his attention to the menu. The restaurant had an Italian name but that
didn't mean anything, nearly every restaurant in Sofia served
pizza, and nearly all of them offered the same dozen or so
Bulgarian dishes, meat and vegetables and eggs, or all of them
I could afford. R. studied every page, and then he ordered

what he always did, pointing to it mutely with a smile as he angled the menu toward the waitress: a salad of greens and strips of eggplant covered in a sweet dressing that he loved. We handed over our menus, and then R. turned his face to the glass beside us, watching the wind, which was visible both in the detritus it carried, papers and leaves and the little plastic cups coffee comes in here, and in the resistance of everything fastened down. Already the last of the light was fading, and as much as the world outside it was R.'s face I saw, which was pensive as he said again it was a crazy wind.

But he was bright-faced when he turned back to me and I shifted my gaze from his reflection to the real image. He asked me about my day, and I told him something funny, I don't remember what, something at my own expense; he liked stories in which I was a little ridiculous, in which students got the best of me. It had the effect I wanted, which was his laugh, or less his laugh than the transformation his face underwent when he smiled. It isn't true, what I said earlier, really I think I was caught from our first meeting, or even before our meeting, from the first photographs he sent me that showed his face. We had been chatting for several days by then, emailing back and forth on a dating site, though it wasn't for dating so much as for sex, which at first was all we thought we wanted. And anyway he was twenty-one, too young to take seriously; it might be a bit of fun, I thought when I looked at his profile, a bit of fun but nothing more. His pictures didn't show very much, mostly his torso, which was thick and unsculpted, a little heavy in a way I liked. In his second email he sent a link to a video that showed what most men must have wanted to see: he was naked, exposing himself, turning to give a full view before he jerked himself off. There was something dispiriting about it, the faceless body too starkly displayed, turning as if on a dais; it shamed me a little to enjoy it. He waited several days before he showed me more, and only after I had promised to be discreet; he wasn't out, he told me, not even to his closest friends, and so it was a pledge of trust to send the photo in which finally I saw his face. He was at a club, there were other people behind him in the dark, but he was the only one looking at the camera. The glare of the flash was bright on his skin, and he seemed gripped by joy, there's no other way to say it, his eyes were shut and his mouth stretched impossibly wide, revealing teeth that were large and imperfect, an upper one in front just slightly skewed. When I saw it I knew I wanted to be smiled at like that. I would never get tired of it, I thought in the restaurant, each time he smiled it filled me with a happiness I had never felt before, a happiness that was particularly his to give.

He told me about his day then, which was less regimented than mine, the day of a student. He was in Sofia as part of a program that shuttled college students around the EU, an attempt to stitch up the union though in R.'s case it hadn't worked; he hated Bulgaria, he said, almost as much as he hated his own country. He had come with M., a friend from his university in Lisbon. He had thought it would be good to know someone here but it wasn't good, he felt watched, forced to compromise and deceive, stuck with the self he would have liked to leave behind; that was really what he hated, I thought, not the country he lived in but the life he had made there. He was studying physical therapy, though he had wanted to major in languages, he told me the first time we met, when we talked for hours in a café before he came home with me. His parents insisted that he study something practical, a trade, but nothing's practical now, he had said, laughing bitterly, there aren't any jobs for anybody in Portugal, I should have studied what I wanted. He had a talent for languages; his English was almost perfect, natural and easy, and when he learned I was a teacher, he said with something like pride that he had always done well in his literature classes in high school, which were the only classes he enjoyed. When we got to my apartment that first time, before we moved into the bedroom, while we were still taking pleasure in delay, he recited a poem to me in his own language, a few lines of Pessoa he said everyone learned in school. It could have been anything, I didn't understand a word of it, but it charmed me and allowed me to reach for him, to pull him close and press my mouth to his.

In Bulgaria he was studying at the National Sports Academy, though that wasn't the kind of therapy he wanted to do; he wanted to help people, he said, real people with real problems, not athletes with sore muscles. But today at least there had been a change of routine, he told me as we waited for our food; instead of practicing the techniques on each other, members of one of the teams had come in, they stripped to their briefs and laid themselves out on the tables. My guy was so beautiful, R. said, he wasn't too big like some of the others, and I got to spend half an hour just touching him. I had to be careful, he went on, lowering his voice enough that I had to lean forward to hear him, I didn't want anyone to see how much I liked him. I was so scared I would touch him wrong, I'm sure it was an awful massage. And he didn't speak any

English, so he couldn't tell me how anything felt, I just kept asking him okay? okay? until the teacher told me to stop. It was kind of hot, he said, looking up at me, and something he saw made him smile. Are you jealous, he asked, and I denied it too quickly, though it wasn't exactly jealousy I felt. It made me worry we had different ideas about the story we were living together; I would tell that to a friend, not a lover, and it was as though R. had heard this thought when he continued. I've never had anybody to talk to about this, he said, you're the only one, and then he smiled again. But I like that you're jealous, he said, it's nice, nobody's ever been jealous of me before, and again he made that gesture with his fingers that was like a caress, or the idea of a caress. But he snatched his hand back quickly, almost guiltily, as the waitress set down our food, saying first *Zapovyadaite*, here you are, and then, more extravagantly, *da vi e sladko*, may it be sweet to you, a kind of courtesy that was out of place in such a casual restaurant. I glanced up as I thanked her, and in the moment before she turned away I thought I caught a look on her face that was something more than politeness, a look that was kind, and I wondered whether she had seen R.'s gesture and read it rightly and given it, in this small way, a kind of blessing.

R. had already turned his attention to his food, salting it and then rotating his plate until its arrangement pleased him. I loved to watch him eat, which he did with a kind of joyful absorption, and I left my pizza untouched as I watched him lift the first bite to his mouth and close his eyes with pleasure, only then returning his attention to me. After class it was a boring day, he said, M. and I went back to our room and slept, but then the Polish girl woke us up, the annoying one, remember, I told you about her. I did remember, though I had forgotten her name; she had pursued R. since they arrived, more and more aggressively, until one night shortly after he and I met he let her take him back to her room. They had been dancing at one of the clubs in Studentski grad, a part of the city named for the many schools and dormitories there, though it was the least studious quarter in Sofia, full of discotheques and casinos and bars; it was where my own students spent their weekends. R. told me this story at our second meeting, while we were lying in bed together, an intimacy I was surprised to find I wanted; usually after sex I was eager to be alone. I was drunk, he said, but that wasn't why I went, I wanted to know if I liked it, I've only ever been with guys but I thought maybe I like girls too, I wanted to try. They had kissed and taken off their clothes and lain down together, he told me, and he didn't respond at all; it was awful, he said, even when she gave me a blowjob I couldn't get hard, it was like I was dead down there. She told me not to worry, I was just too drunk, but that's not true, I can get hard when I'm drunk, I can always get hard. I guess this really is what I am, he said. We had been lying next to each other while he spoke, both on our backs, not touching, but after he said this he rolled toward me and put his hand on my chest, and then he laid his head on top of his hand.

She had stopped by today to remind them of the plans they had made, a whole group was headed to dinner and then out to the clubs; she wanted to talk to me, R. went on, but I said M. was sleeping, I practically closed the door in her face. I don't want to be mean, he said to me, but what does she want, she won't leave me alone. She wants you, I said, trying to laugh, I sympathize; I had intended to be charming, but R. didn't smile. He seemed uneasy, shifting in his seat, he pushed his food around but wasn't eating now. Maybe it was the wind; each time it struck the glass he leaned away from it, and again I thought I had been wrong to sit there, a table in the middle of the room would have been better, we would have been less exposed. And then M. got up, R. said, and when I told him I didn't want to go, that I was tired and would stay home, he started saying he would stay in too, he would study instead. I thought I would lose my mind, R. said, his English turning colloquial as it always did when he was agitated, using phrases he had learned from American sitcoms, I mean Jesus, I'm not his mother, we're not married, he can do things on his own. M. was always his excuse for our missed dates, and I grew increasingly annoyed as he went on; so much of what he complained about seemed of his own doing, and so easy to change. Portugal was a modern country, it wasn't like Bulgaria, men like us could live openly there, could even marry; surely he only needed a little courage to claim the freedom he said he wanted.

You could just tell him, I said, cutting into R.'s monologue, and though I had said versions of this before he looked up at me blankly. About us, I mean, you could tell him about us, and then you wouldn't have to lie. He made an exasperated sound at this, a dismissive sound that made me angry, or not angry, quite, but annoyed. Listen, I said, wouldn't it be better, isn't it what you want? I knew I should probably stop but I went on, I want you to be happy, I said, really happy, and you can't be happy when you have to lie so much. I fell silent then, as did everyone else in the restaurant, an instant of shock at a gust of wind that smacked angrily at the building, an even stronger gust than the others. It was like being besieged, I thought, as conversations picked up and the room filled again with noise, a little tentative now, as if we were all embarrassed at having been frightened. R. began to speak but I had more I wanted to say, I spoke over him, Wait, I said, let me just, and then I paused again, at a loss. You're happy when you're with me, right, I said, and he made his noise of exasperation again, a glottal exhalation. You know I am, he said, and it was true, it was something we had already begun to say to each other, that we made each other happy. This was true for me from the very first evening, after I had drawn him to me and kissed him and we fell into bed together, when I looked up at him in the dark and saw his smile. Sex had never been joyful for me before, or almost never, it had always been fraught with shame and anxiety and fear, all of which vanished at the sight of his smile, simply vanished, it poured a kind of cleanness over everything we did. He had given me so much, I thought, for all that he couldn't give, and I was ashamed of the tone I had taken. I do know, I said, speaking more gently now, and you know I'm happy too, and maybe the best thing this could do, I meant our friendship, relationship, I didn't know what word to use, is show you what it would be like if you were open, if you let yourself live in a fuller way. I could see that my speech wasn't having the effect I wanted, that R.'s mood was turning darker; he wasn't looking at me anymore but at the window, at his reflection or the world beyond it. I should have stopped talking but I couldn't stop, I want you to be able to live, I said, really live, I don't want you to just wait for things to happen to you, I want you

to be happy. And what are you afraid of, I asked, do you really think your friends won't accept you, your parents? His
family wasn't religious, I knew, he was from a small place
but not a particularly conservative one. I think you should
trust them more, I said, I think you should trust that they
love you.

Stop, he said. He was still looking at the window, not
at his own reflection but at something in the far distance,
though there wasn't a far distance, there was just the garden
wall invisible in the dark. Just stop, he said, you don't know
what you're talking about, and when he turned his gaze to
mine I could see he was angry. You're talking to me like a
child, he said, I'm not a child, you can't talk to me like that.
I'm sorry, I said quickly, meaning it, I didn't want you to
feel that, really, I'm sorry. He was silent then, he turned back
to the window, as though there were something to see there,
and I thought I could see him let go of his anger, all at once,
his shoulders slumped a little as it went. The wind continued
its assault, its constant charge against the glass, but R. wasn't
flinching from it anymore, he seemed almost to be leaning
toward the window as he gazed through it, or maybe he was
just leaning away from me.

It's not just that I'm afraid, he said, though I am afraid,
you can say whatever you want but it's scary, I don't want
people to change how they think of me. I know, I started to
say, I didn't mean, but he motioned with his hand to cut me
off. It isn't that, he said after a pause, I mean that's not the
main reason. He paused again, and the noise of the restaurant
rose around us. I hadn't been aware of it for some time, but
now I heard the voices at the other tables, heard without un-

derstanding; they were jumbled, overlapping and indistinct, punctuated suddenly by an eruption of laughter in a far corner. When I was little, R. began, speaking more slowly than I had ever heard him speak, and almost with a different voice, muted and inward, a voice that though it addressed me didn't welcome my company. When I was living in the Azores, he said, it was terrible, there was nothing to do, there were more cows around than people. I had maybe two friends, he said, and we lived so far away from everything I didn't even get to see them very much, I only saw them at school. There were my sisters, but they were older, they didn't want anything to do with me, and my parents—I don't know, they were fine, I know you say I care too much about what they think but we've never been close, I'm not really sure they think about me all that much. All I did was watch TV, stupid cartoons or American shows, it was the only thing to do. There was only one person I was close to, and he wasn't my friend, he was older, a friend of my father's. We had known him forever, we called him uncle but he wasn't our uncle, he was just my father's friend. He was always nice, he would talk to me and ask me things and listen to me, he was the only person who made me feel like I was interesting. He was at our house a lot, he'd come over for dinner, and I was always happy to see him, more than happy, excited; I guess I had a crush on him, I don't know, I didn't think of it like that. When I was older, twelve or thirteen, we would go on walks while my mother was making dinner. It sounds weird now but it didn't feel weird, my parents thought it was good for me, and it was for a while, I think, R. said, I mean I was happy. There was a place we used to go, near the American base, a field with a big concrete shell of a building. I don't know what it was exactly, it was like a mall, there were three floors but only the skeleton, nothing else; it was something they started to build a long time ago and didn't finish. It was a place to walk, and to do other things; there were always bottles and cans and cigarettes, people hung out there, I guess, there was nowhere else to go. Guys went there too, R. said; I didn't know it then, we were only there in the daytime, but at night it was a cruising place, and when I got older it was where I went too, even though I hated it. It was always the same three or four married assholes, but whatever, it was something. We'd go walking there, just talking to each other, and then one day he stopped and pointed at something on the ground. It was a condom somebody had dropped by one of the walls, stretched out and dry, it was disgusting. He pointed at it with his shoe and asked me if I knew what it was for. And that's how he started it, R. said, he put his arm around me and led me behind one of the walls where no one would see us. I didn't want it but I let him do it, I guess, I mean I didn't fight him and I never said anything, I let it happen. R. looked at me then, finally turning away from the glass, he looked at me where I sat immobile as he spoke, my fork still in my hand. I never said anything, he repeated, I've never said anything until now. Oh, I said, the single syllable, not a word but a sound, oh, and I set my fork down beside the plate I had hardly touched, that was past touching now. *Skupi*, I said, I'm sorry, I'm so sorry, but at this his anger snapped back, a fierce anger as he said See, almost snarling it, you see me differently now, I don't want you to be sorry for me, I don't want to be some hurt little boy, I don't want it. On his face there was an expression I had never seen before, on his face or any other, it was a desperate, frightened face, though frightened of what I wasn't sure. Okay, I said, leaning back, I was frightened too, okay.

He turned away from me again and took a deep breath. The point isn't to make you feel sorry, he said more calmly, looking at the night and the wind that filled it, the point is that I'm not just scared, that's not the only reason I don't want to tell people what I am. If I was open, he said, looking at me, it would be like saying what he did to me was okay, it would be like accepting it. I don't know if I was like this before, probably I was, probably he saw I was and thought I wanted it; and maybe I did want it, maybe that's why I never said anything, maybe I let it happen because I wanted it. I don't know, he said, that's the problem, how can I know what I wanted then, before he did it, how can I know what's me and what's what he did to me? I know it's stupid, but what if he made me this way, how can I be proud of it then, he said, how can I march in some fucking parade, maybe that's fucked up but it's what I feel. He stopped suddenly, as if he had just realized how loudly he was speaking; he looked around but no one was paying us any mind. Can we go now, he said, please, I don't want to eat anymore. Yes, I said, of course, and I scanned the room for our server, catching her eye and making a little motion in the air to signal for our check. Was everything all right, she said when she brought it, gesturing to our half-eaten meals, and I said it was, thank you, we were just ready to go, and I gave her a too-large tip, not wanting to wait for my change. R. was already pulling on his coat, wrapping his scarf around his neck, bundling himself up as

I rose. He was eager to get away from what he had said, I thought, and I worried it wasn't only the place he was fleeing but me, too, that now I would show him an image of himself he hated. There was so much I wanted to say to him but he didn't give me the chance, he had gotten up too quickly, and now he was moving away with his back to me; I would have had to call out to him as I rose from my seat, which of course I couldn't do in the crowded restaurant, though I wanted to call or reach out to him, to catch him and draw him near. I followed as he made his way between the tables, and then he paused for me to join him before he shoved open the door.

Immediately we were in it, the rush and moil of wind that dragged at us and snatched our breath; I couldn't have called out to him now, I had to duck my chin into my coat to breathe. We leaned into the wind as we made our way to the boulevard, squinting against the grit it carried, whether African sand, or, as I imagined, the grime of the streets. We were walking against it, kicking the trash it swept toward us. It's a filthy city, though every morning an army of red-vested women descends with brooms and metal pails to scour the streets, endlessly and to no avail. We walked side by side, but it was R. who led the way, he strode as if taking no account of me. At the Sakharov intersection I thought he might turn toward the metro, putting an end to our evening and maybe to more than our evening; it was easy to imagine him slipping away from me into that life where I had no place. Of course I had no claim on him, our entire relationship was founded on claimlessness, and I was frightened to realize how much I would care if he turned, I would be devastated, how had I let myself feel so much. But he didn't turn, he passed Sakharov and began to cross the parking lot of the supermarket that bordered the tangle of streets in which I lived, Mladost 1A, the name a remnant of the Communist order indecipherable now in the mess of new buildings. The market was nearly empty, it was late, almost closing time, but the automatic glass doors were sliding open and shut, open and shut, though no one was coming in or out; it was something to do with the wind, I thought, the disorder it made of everything. I was glad he was coming home with me, but it meant I would have to have something to say to him, when we were out of the wind and together again in my room, in the bed where we had said so much to each other—it wasn't true that I had no claim on him, I thought, each word was a claim, his words and mine—and now all I had wanted to say seemed false, or if not false then irrelevant. Of course it wasn't his fault, I would say, of course he was blameless, entirely blameless; there wasn't any invitation he could have given, even if he had wanted it there wasn't any permission he could give. But none of this was right, I rejected the phrases even as they formed, not just because they were objectionable in themselves but because none of them answered his real fear, which was true, I thought: that we can never be sure of what we want, I mean of the authenticity of it, of its purity in relation to ourselves.

Just past the grocery there was a wide trench where they were extending the metro across Mladost, tearing open whole segments of pavement a few hundred meters at a time, and along the length of it was a simple chain fence, draped in green plastic mesh, the metal poles anchored in plastic buckets filled with concrete. It was meant as a deterrent but really it would have been easy to get through, the blocks weren't heavy, with a little effort you could shift them. Work had been stopped for days, it was too dangerous in the wind, and when we came to the fence we saw that one of the poles had tipped over; the wind had caught the green mesh and now it hung suspended over the drop, held in place by its neighbors, which for the moment were still upright. Jesus, I heard R. say, or thought I heard it, and we kept our distance as we walked to a segment of unbroken ground where we could cross. And then we were on my street and at my building and the door slammed shut behind us. R. started up the stairs, not waiting for the elevator as we usually did; I only lived on the third floor, but we had made a kind of ritual of it, as soon as the doors closed we kissed and groped each other, half silly and half sincere, pulling apart at the last moment before the doors opened again. But today R. took the stairs, and I followed him, letting him climb ahead of me. He hadn't pressed the switch to set the lights running on their timer and so neither did I, the hallways were dark but there was a dull light from the window at each floor, neon signs and lights from neighboring buildings filtered through the unwashed glass. I could hear noises from the apartments we passed, televisions and voices that mixed with the sound of the wind, and from one there was a quick burst of laughter, a man's voice, joining in the laughter from the show he was watching. R. reached my floor and waited for me at the end of the hallway, where it was truly dark, there wasn't any window to let in light from the street. He slid past me when I opened the door and headed to the bedroom while I locked it again. I hung back, resting my hand on the knob as I heard the familiar sounds of him undressing, fabric pulled off, the heavy buckle of his belt striking the floor, and then the mattress sighing with his weight.

I pulled off my own clothes at the door, I left them and walked to the bedroom naked. He was on his back, one of his arms across his face, as if to block the light from his eyes, though there wasn't any light, or hardly any. The curtains were drawn across the windows, not the heavy drapes but the gauze that obscured the interior from view, my building was surrounded by others, someone might always be watching. I lay down next to him. He was beautiful in the dark, his form a deeper shadow beside me, his olive skin and the dense compactness of him, he was the most beautiful, I thought, as I had thought before. I didn't touch him, we lay silent for a moment until finally I spoke, whispering *Skupi*, are you all right, talk to me, say something; and though he didn't say anything he did make a noise, a small noise of desire or grief, I couldn't tell which, and then he reached over and pulled me to him, my face first and then as we kissed the rest of me, his hands urged me to move until I was on top of him. It felt like passion, his mouth and his hands on me, it felt like the hunger I was still amazed I could arouse in him. He pressed his pelvis into me, making me feel that he was hard, as I was, his eyes were squeezed shut and his face wore an expression I couldn't read, and then I pressed down and his lips parted and he made a sound that was unmistakably of pleasure, I thought. He pulled my face to his again, he slid his tongue into my mouth and drew out my own, which he caught with his lips and teeth, biting it almost to the point of pain. All the while he was making a sound I had never heard from him before, a series of short moans, almost pants, and as we kissed and pressed against each other he lifted his knees up on either side of me, as if to wrap them around me, as if to embrace me with all four of his limbs, though that's not what he did, instead he shifted his hips up. I was confused, it was a reversal of our roles, I had never fucked him before, but when I whispered Are you sure the strange sounds he made intensified, in frequency and volume both. I lifted myself off him and reached to the side table to take a condom from the drawer, but as I tore the little package with my teeth I heard R. say No, and when I said What, taken aback, he said it again, more clearly, No, and though I hesitated I set it aside. Since we had met he had been my only partner, he was the only partner I wanted, but it was a risk, I knew, neither of us could be sure the other was safe, and maybe the risk was part of my excitement, of course it was. Though it wasn't my usual role or a role I usually enjoyed I was eager for it, more than eager, I was surprised by what I felt as I slicked myself with lubricant from the same drawer, hissing a little at the cold of it; and then I applied it to R., between the legs he had raised. I would take my time, I would be gentle, otherwise it would be difficult for him, I thought, I mean more difficult. But he didn't want me to take my time, Go on, he said, I'm ready, drawing his legs up farther to make room for me. But he wasn't ready, when I entered him he cried out, a terrible sound. I stopped but only briefly, since he said again Go, at least that's what I thought he said, go, and I pressed farther into him, drawn forward by what he had said and by my own pleasure, which was exquisite; I had never fucked anyone bare before, there was a heat and silkenness in it I had never felt. R. had covered his face with his arm again, I couldn't read his expression as I began to move, and really I was marveling so much at my own feeling that for a moment I neglected his. Anyway he was hiding it, that was why he had covered his face, to hide from me what he felt. I lowered my own face to the arm beneath which he hid, to the pit of his arm; I loved the smell of him, and tonight beside the familiar scent there was something else, his endurance, maybe, his response to pain, since pain was what his noises meant, or some of his noises. When I pressed into him there was a grunt of pain and when I drew out a little sound of need, an invitation or demand that I return, so that if it was pain it was pleasure too, or anyway satisfaction. I liked that I could make him feel this, I found myself seeking new angles to make him feel more, need and satisfaction and pain, it was like a new intimacy, though maybe there was something cruel in it as well, some cruelty in myself I sensed the shape of, a shape I had sensed before but never before with R. I would give him what he wanted, I thought, though whether I was giving something or taking it away I wasn't sure.

There was a sudden noise then, a dull crack that startled me, that startled R., too; both of us tensed as the room was filled with wind, with the noise of it and its force, it made the curtains billow, I felt it cold along my back. The window beside the bed had come open; there was a way to turn the handle that let it tilt in a few inches at the top, it must have come unlatched. The wind made a kind of accompaniment as I began to move again, a rhythm against which I moved, and as I continued fucking R. I thought of the distance from which it had come, though maybe it doesn't make sense to think of it as having any origin at all, maybe it was pure circulation, picking things up and setting them down again willy-nilly, not just broken things but also things that seem whole, the sands of Africa or Greece; it was moving the very lands, I thought, however slowly, nothing was solid, nothing would stay put, and I held on more tightly to R. and drove into him more fiercely, drawing from him those noises of pain and of need, noises maybe of pleasure too. I wanted to root into him, even as the wind said all rootedness was a sham, there were only passing arrangements, makeshift shelters and poor harbors, I love you, I thought suddenly in that rush that makes so much seem possible, I love you, anything I am you have use for is yours.

THE FROG KING

It was too early for there to be so much light, so that when I woke my first thought was of snow. We had pulled the drapes before sleeping but they did almost nothing to darken the room, the snow caught scraps from streetlamps and neon and cast them back up. It was bright enough to see R. still sleeping beside me, cocooned in the blanket I had bought after the first night we spent together, when I woke shivering to find him bound tight in the comforter we were sharing, swaddled beside me. He repeated the word all that day, apropos of nothing, swaddled, swaddled, he had never heard it before, the sound of it made him laugh. He would sleep for hours still, if I let him he would sleep the whole day. He loved to sleep in a way I didn't, sliding into it at every chance, whereas almost always I slept poorly, uneasily, I woke finally with a sense of relief. He complained if I woke him—I'm on holiday, he would say, let me sleep—but he complained more if I let him sleep too long. We only had ten days together, his winter vacation, which he had decided to spend in Sofia while everyone else he knew went home. Mornings were my time to work, to spend with my books and my writing, my time to be alone; I would get up soon but for now I kept looking at him, his face bearded and dark, smoothed out by sleep. It was all I could do not to touch it, as I did often when he was awake, cupping his cheek in my palm or reaching around the curve of his skull. He had shaved his head at the end of the semester, I liked to run my hand around and around it until he ducked and told me to stop, annoyed but laughing, too; even annoyance was part of the pleasure we took in each other, we were that early in love.

I was still groggy with sleep when I turned into the main room, and I stood uncomprehending for a moment before I realized that R. had rearranged things in the night. He had moved the table to the middle of the room, and had placed my winter boots on top of it, beside the little tree we had bought earlier that week. Sticking up from the boots there were packages wrapped in newspaper, his Christmas gifts for me; he must have hidden them somewhere after he arrived, he must have gotten out of bed in the night, careful not to wake me, he must have been quiet as he moved the furniture. I caught my breath at it, I felt a weird pressure and heat climb my throat. I felt like my heart would burst, those were the words for it, the hackneyed phrase, and I was grateful for them, they were a container for what I felt, proof of its commonness. I was grateful for that, too, the commonness of my feeling; I felt some stubborn strangeness in me ease, I felt like part of the human race.

HE HAD SEEN SNOW for the first time that winter, and he loved to be out in it, to stand with his arms outstretched as it fell, his mouth open to the sky. We went out that afternoon, the snow already tracked through but still lovely; the streets were quiet for the holiday, all the shops were closed. We were wearing the scarves I had found when I opened the presents under the tree, which were long and knit in the same pattern, one yellow and one blue; we wouldn't ever be boyfriends who wore the same clothes, R. said, but one shared thing was acceptable, having one shared thing was nice. We didn't go far, just halfway down the block, where I whistled, a short upward swoop I repeated three times, the usual signal. She might not be here, I had said, she isn't always, she goes other places or maybe somebody takes her in, but she came quickly enough from her usual spot around the back of the building. She was beautiful in her way, tawny and medium-sized like most of Sofia's street dogs, too skinny and with mange along one side. She was happy to see us, I thought, happy as she always was to get attention, though she lacked the confidence of some of the other dogs; she stayed near the wall, wagging her tail but not coming too close at first. Even when she let us pet her she tried to keep her distance, cringing in a sidling motion that brought her body within our reach but kept her head angled away, a mixture of eagerness and fear. Somebody had taught her that, I thought, somebody had beaten her, or many people had, but not in this neighborhood, here everyone was kind to her, she was a sort of communal pet. She lost some of her shyness when R. pulled the packet of treats out of his coat pocket, clumsy in his mittens, which he had to take off before he could tear open the packet and pull out one of the strips of leathery meat. She started whining when she saw it, prancing closer, and he crooned her name, Lilliyana,

though that didn't mean anything to her, it was just a name
he had invented, it suited her, he thought. *Ela tuka*, he said,
a phrase I had taught him, come here, and he held out the
treat so she could take it, which she did by stretching her
neck and pulling back her lips, taking hold of it with her front
teeth, like a deer plucking a leaf. He had bought the treats the
night before, when we were buying supplies; she should have
Christmas dinner too, he said. She let us pet her more vigorously then, finally coming close, even pressing her side against
his legs as she begged for a second piece, which he gave her,
though that was all for today, he told her, there would be
more tomorrow. She seemed to accept this, she didn't keep
begging once we turned away, as most dogs would have, I
thought; she disappeared behind the building again to whatever shelter she had found.

WE FOUND THE TREE by chance one late afternoon. We
were in a part of town I'd never seen before, on the other
side of the city center, looking for a German supermarket, a
chain that was popular in Western Europe but that had only
the single store in Sofia. It was less a store than a warehouse,
really, there weren't shelves but huge bins people pawed
through, everything mixed together, a dozen kinds of chocolate bars in one bin, toothpaste and shaving cream in another. The chain had its own brand of food, and R. was craving
something from his life in Lisbon, a frozen lasagna, and when
we found it in an oversized freezer case he clutched it to his
chest with happiness. It was a long walk from the store to

the metro, longer because the sidewalks were caked with ice. R. scolded me as we walked, telling me to take my hands out of my pockets, to keep them free in case I slipped, as for whatever reason I did often enough; if it had been night he would have passed his arm through mine to keep me upright. R. saw the trees first, in the window of a little shop that was full of Christmas decorations. Even from outside you could see how cheap they were, all metal wire and plastic bristles, but R. insisted that we needed one, and ornaments, a box of lights; I want to have a real Christmas, he said. It was maybe three feet tall, it hardly weighed anything but it was cumbersome, I held it in both arms like a child as we walked. I felt a little ridiculous sitting with it on the train but R. seemed proud, he kept one arm around it to hold it steady on the seat between us. When we got home, he wanted to trim the tree right away, and he opened the box of tinsel to find that it was far too large, we hadn't been paying attention, it was meant for a much bigger tree. He laughed as he wrapped it again and again around the branches; she was swaddled now, he said, it would keep her warm. Her, I repeated back to him, inquisitive, mocking him a little, and this gave him an idea: she needed a name, he said, and he decided to call her Madeleine, I don't have any idea where it came from but he loved to say it. He liked to give things names, I think it was a way of laying claim to them, and he called out to her every time he passed, almost singing it, Madeleine, Madeleine. He saved the box of ornaments for Christmas Eve, little glass balls we hung from hooks on the branches, tucked among the tinsel. We knelt to arrange them, and when we finished R. sat back on his heels. Isn't she beautiful, he said, taking my hand in his, but he answered the question himself, she is, isn't she, I think she's beautiful.

WE WENT TO BOLOGNA because it was the cheapest place we could fly: there were tickets for forty euros, a price I could afford. We packed a single carry-on each, anything else would have meant a fee, and rode in a cab to the airport's old terminal, which the budget airlines used. It was my first time leaving the country. During breaks, when the other American teachers left for places near or far—Istanbul, Tangier, St. Petersburg—I stayed behind; I didn't want to travel, I said, I wanted to be settled in a single place. I studied Bulgarian, I read, I wandered the streets downtown. But I did want to travel with R., to leave Sofia, where even when his friends were gone there was a pressure of secrecy, where it was too dangerous to hold hands in the streets, to kiss in public, however chastely, where everywhere we had to keep a casual distance; I wanted to be with him in a place where we could be freer with each other, a place in the West. It was my gift to him, a getaway, a bit of romance. We arrived at the airport early enough to be first in line for the unassigned seats, and sat in the front row, where there was extra room for our legs. Even so my knees almost touched those of the single attendant who sat facing us, strapped into her foldout seat. She spoke English with an accent I couldn't place, not Bulgarian but something Eastern European, and she smiled slightly, kindly I thought, when the plane started down the runway, thrusting us all back, and R. moved his hand to cover mine where it lay on my knee.

WE BOOKED THE CHEAPEST HOTEL, too, a chain a good way from the city center, with a bus stop outside for getting to town. We arrived too late for any exploring, we'd have to wait until morning to see the city. It was hard not to feel depressed by our room, which had the corporate airlessness of such places, comfort sterilized of any human touch. It was on the second floor, overlooking the parking lot. It's not exactly a dream of Italy, I said, meaning it as an apology, but R. laughed, he drew the curtain across the glass and pulled me to the bed. Who cares about the view, he said, the bed is nice, that's all that matters, you should care about the bed, and then we were both laughing, one on top of the other.

The hotel's one luxury was the breakfast we found the next morning, a buffet of eggs and sliced meats, yogurt and fruit, a table overloaded with cakes and tarts. It was early still—we had set our alarms, we wanted the whole day for the city—and I needed coffee first, which meant a complicated machine with a digital screen, then waiting for the paper cup to fill. When I turned back, I saw that R. had covered our table with little plates, a sample from each of the sweets. He hadn't left any room for me, and I waited while he tried to clear a space for my coffee, shifting the plates around until one almost tipped onto the floor, he caught it just in time. I made a little noise, exasperated and amused, and he looked up at me and shrugged. He would take a single bite from each plate, then move it to one side or the other, sorting out the things he liked. I watched him for a while, and then Skups, I said, my tone half question, half disbelief, making a gesture that took in the table with its plates, the room, the other people eating. He shrugged again, glancing around at the assortment of other travelers, businessmen mostly, a few couples. Who cares, he said, using his fork to dig into another piece of something, they don't know me, we'll never see them again, why should I care what they think?

I remembered this later, waiting for the bus that would take us to town. We were the only people in the little shelter at the stop, huddling together against the wind, which was sharper than I had expected; it wasn't very cold but it was cold enough for our coats, for the scarves we had draped around each other before heading out. Then R. stepped up onto the bench, he grabbed my shoulders and turned me to face him. Now I'm the taller one, he said, and bent down to kiss me, not a chaste kiss, he gripped my hair and tilted my head farther back to probe my mouth with his tongue. I tried to pull away, laughing: it was a busy road, we were in full view of the passing cars. But he held me tight, kissing me with urgency, until I realized that exposure was the point, that he wanted to show off, here where nobody knew him, where he could be anonymous and free, could live out an ideal of candor. He leaned into me, pressing his pelvis into my stomach so I felt his cock hard between us; it turned him on to show off like this, I had had no idea. I gripped him, using my body to shield us, I gripped him hard with both my hands through his jeans. I started to undo his belt, wanting to meet him in his daring, to show him I was game; and he moaned into my mouth before he pulled back and pushed my hand away. *Porta-te bem*, he said, slapping my face lightly and laughing, behave.

THE BUS LEFT US in the Piazza Maggiore, where there was a huge wooden statue in the center of the square, a cylinder painted an uneven green. The bottom half was featureless, the top carved into the torso of a frog, regal and upright, his lips drawn back in an expression at once benevolent and severe. Two arms crossed at his stomach, four long fingers hanging down from each; above the half-lidded eyes there was a crown with four prongs. Cables stretched down from its midsection, securing it to the pavement; wooden barriers marked off a space around it. It would be burned, the man working at reception told us back at the hotel when we asked, it was the tradition, the old year burned at the turn of the new. I remembered something I had seen in a movie, Fellini maybe, a stuffed witch on a pile of kindling and old furniture, the trash of the past, the promise of an uncluttered future. I wondered why we didn't do it in the States, where we love to pretend to start afresh, where we love to burn things down. There was nothing like it in Bulgaria either, where New Year's was celebrated at home; families gathered in apartments and at midnight they set off fireworks from their balconies. It had frightened me my first year, the sound ricocheting off the walls as the little bombs fell into the streets below, where everyone knew not to be, they were impassible for a good half hour. Which was the opposite of clearing away: all over the city the explosions came down and nobody swept them up, the wrappers and casings littered the streets until the heavy spring rains. It wasn't a traditional statue, the man told us, there was a competition each year, artists submitted designs and the winner had his work displayed there, in the center of the city, for a week before it was burned. For us the frog is a symbol, the man said, it means poverty, here in Bologna, in Italy, so it means to burn poverty. You know the crisis is very hard here, he said, the austerity is very hard, it would be good to burn it away. He had apologized for his English, but it was very good, less stiff than he seemed in his jacket and tie; he was young, midtwenties, a college student in a university town. You should go, he said, it's a party, there will be music and lots of people and you can watch the fire, it's something you should see.

THERE WAS SO MUCH TO SEE, too much; I walked around in a daze of looking. We moved in and out of churches crowded with paintings, huge and smoke-darkened, the ceilings crammed with color, I got tired of trying to see them. R. was full of zeal, he wanted to see everything—who knows when we'll be back, he said. The dilemma of vacations, the exhaustion of the last chance. Everything became unremarkable, nothing moved me, it was all a blur of perfection. I wanted to get the bus back to the hotel, I wanted to rest my eyes. But just one more thing, R. said, paging through the guidebook we had bought, and he led me to a small museum, a house converted after the artist who had lived in it had died. There were just a few rooms, open and uncluttered, the walls painted mercifully white; it wouldn't take long for R. to

make his circuit. I followed him, barely looking at the paintings, which were small and unremarkable, or remarkable
only for their plainness. They were quiet and unambitious,
minor, I thought at first, still lifes and modest landscapes,
interesting mostly for having so little to do with everything
else we had seen; the painter had spent his whole life in this
city but seemed indifferent to the examples it offered, to the
virtuousity and gorgeousness it prized. I found myself looking longer, looking more slowly, I let R. walk on ahead. The
same subjects appeared again and again, household objects,
plates and bowls, not filled with flowers or fruit but empty,
set against a plain background. I stopped in front of one that
showed a pitcher and cups, white and gray on a tan surface,
behind them a blue wall. Something held me there looking,
something made me lean in to look more closely. The cups
were mismatched in color and in shape, the pitcher rose oddly
elongated behind them, the whole painting was eccentric,
asymmetrical. There was a kind of presence in the painting, I
felt, I could sense it humming at a frequency I wanted to tune
myself to catch. I liked the seeming naivety of it, the way the
simple figures had been simplified further, purified or ideal-
ized to geometrical forms, almost, but rendered bluntly, im-
perfectly. And the brushstrokes were imperfect too, visible,
haphazard, the paint distributed unevenly, inexpertly; but
that wasn't right, really it was striving for something ideal,
that was what I felt, the frequency I wanted to catch. What
I took at first for blocks of color dissolved when I leaned in,
were modulated, textured, full of movement somehow, not
the movement of objects but of light, which fell across them
gently, undramatically. But that's not right either, it didn't

fall across them, there weren't any shadows; I couldn't locate the light at all, or tell if the scene depicted morning or noon. It was as if the objects emanated their own light, which didn't move from one quadrant of the painting to another, as real light would, but vibrated somehow, giving a sense of movement and stillness at once. There was a promise in it, I felt, I mean a promise for me, a claim about what life could be.

VENICE WAS TWO HOURS AWAY by train, another unmissable chance. We wouldn't stay the night, the hotel in Bologna was already paid for, we would spend a few hours exploring and then come back. On the train I stared at the fields we passed, which were laid out neatly, in lines I realized I had never seen in Bulgaria; the fields alongside the train from Sofia to the coast were shaggy, inexactly drawn, like the fields I remembered from my childhood, my family's fields in Kentucky, nothing like this clean geometry. I stared at them, hypnotized, and turned away only when I felt R.'s hand on my ankle, calling me back. We were facing each other, I had my foot on the empty seat beside him, and he had hooked his fingers underneath the cuff of my jeans and was stroking me softly, privately, not looking up from his book. But I knew he wasn't reading, he was smiling just slightly, his eyes on the page, he was basking in how I looked at him.

WE HAD NO PLANS IN VENICE, had done no research. But it didn't matter, just to be there was enough, amid the capillary water and sinking stone; there was a kind of uniform beauty to

everything, a blanket wonder. Every corner we turned made
R. gasp, every church we stepped into, every statue with its
marble frothed up like surf, like the involutions of thought.
Fuck these people, R. whispered as we stared at a painted ceiling, fuck them for getting to live in a place like this. He was
smiling when I glanced at him but I knew he meant it, or
half meant it. He often said that he was born in the wrong
place; shitty Portugal, he would say, shitty Algarve, the shitty
Azores, shitty Lisbon, it should all have been different, his
life was fucked. Sometimes I could bring him out of these
moods, I could kiss him and say he had a new life now, his life
with me, who knew where we'd end up, in Europe or America, who knew what adventures we'd have, and sometimes
he pushed me away or turned his face from mine. We don't
get to choose anything, he'd say then, we think we do but
it's an illusion, we're insects, we get stepped on or we don't,
that's all. When he talked like this there was nothing I could
do, anything I did made it worse, whether I got angry or sad
or tried to make him feel my own happiness, the happiness I
felt so often just looking at him, as he slept or read, or stared
into the screen of his laptop. It was an immovable force, this
mood that descended on him sometimes, and I worried that it
was descending on him now, that it would darken the rest of
our day. But it didn't descend. When we left the church and
turned blindly around the next corner he pulled me into an
alcove and kissed me, his hands on the side of my face. I can't
believe I'm here, he said, it's like a movie, I'm in Venice with
my American boyfriend. He laughed. My sister would be so
jealous, she's always wanted an American boyfriend, and I got
one first. And then he was off again, dragging me by the hand

behind him. He did this repeatedly, pulling me into door-
ways and alleys to kiss me, always somewhere a little apart,
though we were still noticed, people passing would stare at
us or look decidedly away. One heavy old man scowled; a
young couple laughed, which I minded more. R. seemed
not to notice but I noticed, it was a weird reversal: he was
the more open one here, and I was hyperaware, feeling the
reflexes of fear though I wasn't afraid, I didn't think I was
afraid.

Our only principle was to stay away from the crowds of
other tourists who moved in migratory flocks, following the
little pennant or flag the guides all held above their heads,
tiny bright triangles on long stems. It meant not seeing the
important things but I didn't care, their edges were rubbed
smooth by too much looking, there was nothing for my attention to catch on in them. I liked the dark streets we turned
into better, the narrow paths beside the canals. Even here
there were restaurants and shops, nowhere on that island is
indifferent to tourists, money from elsewhere is the blood of
the place. We stopped on the footbridges and looked at the
boats bundled up on either side of the canals, trussed in canvas, their wooden hulls deep shades of blue and green, their
reflections darker shadows in the water. It wasn't late but it
was getting dark already, at least where we were, the sun had
abandoned the narrow alleys to an afternoon dusk. We had
left the grand palazzos behind, the churches; where we were
now there were plastic shopping bags filled with trash beside the doors. This is where the people live, R. said, a trick
of English making him sound like a revolutionary. Then he
laughed and pointed ahead, at a bright yellow bag with the

letters BILLA on it, its red handles tied off in a bow. It was the store we went to all the time in Mladost, our neighborhood store. I knew it was a big chain, that you could find them everywhere in Europe, and still it felt like a bit of good fortune to stumble across it here.

R. pulled out his guidebook then, with its useless maps, he was afraid we would lose the light before we saw San Marco. He started walking more quickly while I hung back, protesting; it didn't matter, everything was beautiful, everything was something we hadn't seen before and wouldn't see again. But he insisted, increasingly frustrated as the map refused to align with the streets we walked; he was better with maps than I was but not by much. He got annoyed with me for walking too slowly and stopping too often, but I wanted to take photos of everything, the buildings, the canals, the laundry hung out in the damp air to dry, the mask shop with its window of carnival grotesques, backlit through the metal grill that had been pulled down. R. was growing frantic in a way I didn't understand. We would lose the light, he kept saying, as though he were an artist imagining a scene, I want to see it before we lose the light. So I put away my camera and walked more quickly, I kept my eyes on R. to avoid being distracted by anything else. And he did find it, finally, by luck mostly, I think, suddenly we turned and it opened out before us, after the cramped alleys the expanse of the square, beyond it the horizon of water. R. turned to me, smiling, and surely it wasn't at that moment that the bells began to ring, it's a trick of memory to stage it that way, but it is how I remember it, the birds flying up, everyone turning to the Campanile, as we did, its top still bright as it caught the last of the sun.

Merchants were walking through the crowds, hawking toys for children, spinning tops that burst into LED color as they helicoptered up. All that was new there was evanescent, the toys, the tourists, R. and I; all that was lasting was old, worn dull with looking though still I wondered to look at it, the centuries-old basilica, the bells, the gold lion on its pedestal, the sea that would swallow it; and everywhere also the books I had read, so that look, there, I could almost convince myself of it, Aschenbach stepping from uncertain water to stone.

I HAD A MIND FULL of useless things, I had always thought, or useless since graduate school, where they had been a kind of currency, the old stories and stray facts that were all that remained of the years in which I had wanted to be a scholar. The books I had read! But in the churches of Venice I found a use for them, I could read the paintings for R., or not the paintings but the stories they told: Joseph of Arimathea, Mary and Martha, Sebastian nursing his arrows. In churches in Bulgaria the paintings were more or less mute to me, but here they made a story I could read, and as I told it to him I saw the pleasure R. took in it, the way he looked at me and then at the painting, I loved to see it. I have a crush on teacher, he said, whispering, and then he smiled his smile that meant happiness, his whole face beaming, turning toward the painting now though I knew the smile was for me. Later, back in Bologna, where we arrived on the last train after all the restaurants had closed—we ate shrink-wrapped sandwiches and chocolate, shared a little bottle of prosecco, all of it from a twenty-four-hour shop near the station—he asked me to tell him more, it didn't matter what. Tell me a story, he said, stretched out in bed as I lay beside him, running my hands across his chest and stomach, feeling his cock grow thick when I grabbed it, tell me another story.

I WOKE A FEW HOURS LATER too hot, stifling in the bedclothes. I switched on the lamp beside the bed. R. slept so deeply I never had to worry about waking him on the nights I couldn't sleep, when I spent hours beside him reading or writing. But this time he did wake, or half wake, as I lay with a book propped on my stomach; he turned toward me and linked his arm through mine before settling back into sleep, his face pressed against my shoulder. I looked at him for a long time before going back to my book. They could make a whole life, I thought, surprised to think it, these moments that filled me up with sweetness, that had changed the texture of existence for me. I had never thought anything like it before.

I WANTED TO MAKE him laugh at first, I meant it almost as a joke. We needed to laugh: it had been hard to return to Sofia after our days in Italy, more snow had fallen but by the time we arrived the city had turned gray again, the holidays were over, the cars kicked black sludge from their tires. And now it was his last night in my apartment; in the morning he would gather his things and go back to Studentski grad, his friends would arrive in the afternoon. We would return to our uncertain arrangements, emails and dates that he might break at the

last minute or without any notice at all, those were the condi-
tions, they were non-negotiable. He hated it, he said, he
didn't want to go back to hiding, and throughout the day his
dread had increased and darkened, coloring everything, until
by nighttime he could barely speak, he had folded in on himself as he did sometimes; it was hard for me to reach him, to
have any effect on him at all. We watched a movie sitting side
by side on the couch, I don't remember what it was, something lighthearted, romantic, though he hardly laughed. We
never really watched movies together, it was always a pre-
tense, we would kiss and touch each other and then forget the
movie, but now it was all I could do to get him to kiss me
back. Finally he let me pull him up from the couch, I folded
the computer shut and pulled him half resisting into the bedroom. He resisted less there, standing beside the bed, he
opened his mouth to me, he let me draw him close and press
my pelvis against his. He raised his arms for me to pull his
shirt up and off, and I felt the mood shifting already, it light-
ened as his passivity became a game almost, his passivity and
my insistence as I struggled with the buckle of his belt, the
button on his jeans; I could feel him almost smile as I kissed
him, as he answered me back more in his kisses, his tongue
pressing against mine. I pushed his jeans and underwear
down, breaking our kiss to kneel and hold them at his ankles
while he pulled his legs free, kissing his cock, which wasn't
hard yet, just once before I rose again. He moved to kiss me
again but I pulled away, then shoved him back, not hard, he
could have resisted but he didn't, he fell backward onto the
bed. Onto our bed, I thought, which was what it had become
in those days, not a lonely place but a place that belonged to

both of us, a loving place; it was something I could think to myself but not say out loud. I took off my own clothes quickly and then launched myself on top of him, which made him flinch and laugh, just once and as if against his will. I caught myself with my hands and when he reached out his own hands, bracing them against my chest, I grabbed them one by one at the wrist and pinned them above his head. He made a noise at this, a little growl, interested and interrogative, as I ground against him, his cock harder now, mine fully hard. I lowered my face but dodged his kiss again, teasing him, and instead kissed his collarbone, first one side and then the other, and then the inside of his arm, just below the elbow, where I knew he was ticklish, and then I licked the pit of his arm, slowly, because I loved the taste of him, first the right and then the left, and he growled again. He was harder now, he pressed his hips up against mine, but I lifted myself off him, beyond his reach. He moaned in frustration, he tried to pull his hands free but I held them firm; *Porta-te bem*, I said to him, and then I did kiss him, I put my tongue in his mouth and he sucked at it hard, tasting me but tasting himself, too, that was what he loved, the taste of himself in my mouth. I broke off the kiss and dipped my head to his chest, kissing first one nipple and then the other, which he didn't really like, he tolerated it, and then to go farther I had to let go of his wrists, which didn't matter, he kept them obediently above his head. I kissed his ribs and then his stomach, always one side and then the other, keeping a symmetrical pattern, keeping it at his pelvis, too, pressing my lips to his right hip and his left but avoiding his cock, moving quickly. He made a noise of complaint but kept his arms where I had left them, still playing our game. He jerked a little when I kissed the inside of his thighs, he was sensitive there, too, but he didn't try to stop me, he was being good, he let me do what I wanted. But I wasn't sure what I wanted, or what I wanted had changed. I had thought I wanted to make him laugh, that after that I wanted sex, but I didn't want sex, I realized, or not only sex. I had let my knees drop off the end of the bed as I moved lower, soon I was kneeling on the floor at the foot of the bed. He was relaxed, more or less, his legs were outstretched, his feet splayed to either side, but his whole body tensed when he felt my lips on the sole of his foot, which he snatched away, I had to grab it and pull it back. He was ticklish there, too, he didn't like to be touched there. It had been a line drawn early on, when it became clear I was more adventurous in sex, had a wider palette of things that turned me on; I hope you're not into that, he had said, laughing, it's gross, I don't want you to be into that. It was a difference between us, that fewer things put me off, that I could be indifferent to something and still indulge it for my partner's sake. That was what he did now, I guess, when he let me pull his foot back to me, holding it in both hands as I kissed the sole again, the arch and then the pads at the base of his toes, each of them, and then the toes themselves. What are you doing, he said, and I couldn't answer, I wasn't sure what I was doing as I took the other foot in my hands and repeated what I had done with the first. I was moving slowly now, the tone had changed; I didn't want to make him laugh anymore, I didn't know what I wanted him to feel. I kissed his ankles next, at three points, moving from the outside in, from right to left on his right leg, from left to right on his left, which

would remain my pattern. Skups, R. said, a question in the
way he said it, his name for me or our name for each other.
But I didn't answer, I made another band of these kisses,
slightly higher than the first, and then another; I would cover
him in kisses, that was what I wanted to do, and I would do
it even though I could feel R.'s impatience, even as he said
again *Skupi*, and then, don't be cheesy, which was his warning against too much affection, against my surfeit of feeling. I
ignored it, moving up another inch. It would take a long time,
I realized; when you imagine something like that you don't
think about how long it will take, how large a body is, how
small a pair of lips. But I would do it, I decided, a kind of un-
hurriedness opened up in me, a weird wide patience I sank
into. I strung kisses across him, his calves and knees, his
thighs, the flesh firm in the center and giving at the sides. They
were places I had never touched him before, some of them,
and this gave gravity to the moment, more gravity; I whispered I love you as I kissed him, and then two kisses later I
whispered it again, which became a new pattern, to whisper it
again and again. His cock was soft when I reached it, as mine
was, I hadn't noticed it until then. I almost passed over it, kissing his upper thigh on the right and then the left, but I didn't
skip it, I kissed it, too, as I had kissed the rest of him, and said
again the words that somehow became more real with repetition. Usually words wear out the more you use them, they
become featureless, rote, and more than any others this is true
of the words I repeated to R.; even in our relationship that was
still so new they had lost most of their flavor. I remembered
the fear I had felt the first time I spoke them to him, weeks
before, when they had had all their force; I had been terrified,

really, not so much that they wouldn't be answered (they weren't, it would be days before he repeated them) as that they would scare him away, that he would startle like the wild thing I sometimes felt he was. But now we said them often, when we left each other and were reunited (even if it was only a room we left, only minutes we were separated). But repeating the words now didn't dull them, it called them to attention somehow, to service, it restored them, and they became difficult to say again; I found myself almost unable to speak as I whispered into R.'s silence, kissing the soft flesh of his stomach, the firmer flesh over his ribs, his nipples and the patch of hair at the center of his chest, his collarbone, the taut skin at his windpipe. His arms were still raised but he had folded them at the elbow, crossing his forearms over his face. I kissed his armpits again, the exposed undersides of his arms, and then (I was kneeling now, my knees on either side of him) I took his arms in my hands and moved them away from his face. He hadn't uttered a sound in all that time, the fifteen or twenty minutes it had taken me to make my way up his body, not since the interrogative of my name, the admonition I ignored; there hadn't been any change in his breath, or none I had noticed, and so I was surprised to see the tears on his face, two lines that fell toward his ears, he hadn't wiped them away. He didn't try to hide them when I moved his arm, or tried only by turning his face slightly, as if he didn't want to meet my gaze (though his eyes were shut, there was no gaze to meet). I paused, wanting to speak, to ask him what they were for, his tears, but I knew what they were for, and so I hung over him a moment before I continued kissing him, the line of his jaw, his chin, his cheek and lips, which didn't answer mine, which suffered themselves to be kissed, his ears, the tracks of his tears, his eyes. It was a kind of blazon of him, of his body, I love you, I whispered again and again to him. And then, when I had laid the last line across his forehead—a garland, I thought, I had garlanded him—You are the most beautiful, I said to him, you are my beautiful boy, and he reached his arms up and pulled me down on top of him, clutching me. You are, he whispered to me, you are, you are.

THEY USED SOME KIND of accelerant, they must have, so that when the three children touched their torches to it (angling their bodies away, keeping the greatest distance between themselves and the fire) the flame leapt up the wood, from the base to the ridiculous crown the whole frog blazed up. And with it there was a huge explosion of sound, air horns and rattlers and little handheld bells children jingled, and above them all human voices, the crowd cheering both the fire and the New Year, which had just struck. There were hundreds of people in the square, pressed tight near the wooden barricades that held them back from the fire but more spread out near the edges, where we were; there was space here for people to toast one another, with wine in plastic cups or little glass bottles like those R. had bought for us, prosecco with a twist-off cap. After we drank I leaned toward him and cupped his face in my palm and we kissed. I moved my mouth in a way he liked, kissing first his upper lip and then his lower before I drew away, hanging my arm around his shoulder. And then, as the statue burned—it was huge, it would take a long time to burn—there was another sound, a salute of drums and a burst of guitars, and then the far corner of the square lit up with floodlights, and there was a new shout from the crowd as it shifted toward the platform where the band had begun to play, four skinny boys bent over their instruments. There was a keyboard as well as the guitars and drums, it was an American sound, I thought, which contrasted with the stone buildings around us, with the pagan fire. R. and I didn't move as the crowd thinned further; we wouldn't stay, it was cold and the band wasn't very good, we would watch the fire a little longer and then go back to the hotel. R. pulled away from me suddenly and reached into his coat pocket, taking from it the packet of raisins he had bought earlier with the wine. I almost forgot, he said, it's almost too late. He handed me his bottle and took off one of his mittens so he could open the packet. Give me your hand, he said, so I put the bottles on the ground and held it out to him, taking my glove off as he asked, and he counted out twelve raisins, placing them in my palm in a single line from my wrist to the tip of my third finger, then counting another twelve for himself. It was the Portuguese tradition, he had told me, a raisin for each month of the year that had passed, a wish for each month of the year to come. He looked at me and smiled, Skups, he said, *feliz ano*, and we kissed again. He ate his all at once, tossing them in his mouth and putting his mitten back on before he leaned down for his bottle and turned to watch the fire. But I didn't watch the fire, I kept my eyes on him, though it was cold and I wanted to be back in the hotel with him, in the warmth of our bed. I took my time, I put the raisins in my mouth one by one, thinking a wish for each, though all my wishes were the same wish.

A VALEDICTION

There was a moment, as the little beaten cab took another tight turn too quickly, when suddenly to our left we could see all at once the three hills of Veliko Turnovo, the houses of the old town clinging to their terraces, the river Yantra snaking its way beneath. I had seen it in precisely this way when I had visited the city a year before, and now R., sitting in the back seat beside me, took a sharp breath at the wonder of it. His fingers found mine as I reached for him across the seat, and we continued looking with our hands linked low, beneath the driver's notice, freed from the weight of uncertainty or sorrow we had carried with us on the train from Gorna Oryahovitsa, a pressure that had almost seemed caused by the trees crowding the tracks, their long branches brushing the clouded glass of our wagon. It was mid-August, nearly the end of summer; R. would be leaving soon. He had come back to Sofia in May, just after finishing his degree in Lisbon, and our idea had been that he would stay, though it was a sacrifice for him to exchange his sun-drunk city, with its river and avenues and tiles, for a city that even in high summer held on to its grayness, like an animal somehow suspicious of the season, unwilling to shed its coat. But R. quickly realized how little there was for him in Sofia, where he had no friends or relatives, and where without the language there was almost no prospect of work, and so what we had thought of as the beginning of real life had become instead an extended vacation, culminating in this final trip together before he went back home.

The road curved toward the town, following the river, and both of us looked down at the water. We had just come from Rousse, a city three hours to the north, where I had finally seen the Danube, the first river I had encountered in Europe on the scale of those I had grown up beside in America. The town had little in the way of a riverfront, just a desolate patch of green like a stain seeping from the city's largest building, a Soviet-era hotel that stood guard on the bank. The river was swollen with summer rains, and we watched the huge weight of it slide silently past, watching too the swallows twisting above us in the darkening air; and then the river was something we felt more than saw, in the darkness it was indistinguishable from the woods on the Romanian bank. There was nothing so impressive about the Yantra, a narrow river so shallow in places it seemed barely to cover its bed; but there was a kind of drama in the winding shape it cut through the land, at one point almost looping back upon itself as it twisted among the hills that gave the city both its character and its purpose. Atop the largest of those hills sat the jagged ruins of Tsarevets, Turnovo's main attraction, a medieval fortress that fell to the Ottomans five centuries ago, a symbol of former greatness that's at once a source of pride and a shadow cast over the present.

A view of Tsarevets, and of the rest of the town from a neighboring hill, was the primary draw of the hotel where the taxi dropped us off. It was a nice hotel, it cost more than I would usually have wanted to pay, but its luxury was like a grand gesture abandoned, the large room with its gorgeous view filled with furniture and linens in various stages of disrepair. Even so, we felt a little flare of happiness on entering it; R. dropped his bags and stepped onto the bed, jumping up and down a few times, and I laughed with him, even as I sensed, just past the edges of what we felt, a hovering dread. It was a habit of mine, to rush toward an ending once I thought I could see it, as if the fact of loss were easier to bear than the chance of it. I didn't want that to happen with R., I struggled against it; he was worth struggling for, I thought, as was the person I found I was with him. Then R. stopped jumping and stood at the foot of the bed, throwing his arms wide, and I stepped toward him for the second half of our ritual of homecoming in these temporary homes; and as I wrapped my arms around his waist and pressed my face to his chest, I felt a flood of relief, the release of something increasingly tightly wound.

We left shortly after, our bags still unpacked, and began to explore the little town. It wasn't like the other tourist towns in Bulgaria; in the shops there were handmade crafts among the mass-produced souvenirs, and in the old town, its vertiginous streets lined with National Revival houses, at first newly renovated but growing more decrepit as we climbed, there were artisans' shops in which men and women looked up hopefully from their work, calling *zapovyadaite*, welcome, come in, to everyone who passed. A year before, the town had been crowded with tourists, their buses nosing through the tiny streets and their bags piled high in lobbies; but now there were few visitors, maybe because it was later in the season and the seaside had drawn them away, and we were often alone as we climbed the steep paths, the cobblestones shifting beneath us. One woman was standing in front of her shop, and beckoned us inside so fervently it would have been difficult to refuse. I glanced at R., who shrugged, and we walked over to her. She spoke to us in English at first, but visibly relaxed when I answered in Bulgarian. My husband speaks perfect English, she said, but he's gone with my son to Sofia for the day, they've left me here alone. The building she welcomed us into was lovely, a two-story house of stone and wood, with cement urns overflowing with flowers at the threshold. The first floor served as a gallery, the walls crowded almost to the ceiling with paintings; others, unhung, leaned in their frames against the walls. I was overwhelmed by the number of them, for a minute I wasn't sure where to look. Please, the woman said, walk around, there are more in the other rooms, and she gestured toward an open doorway to my right. All of them were done by us, she said, we're all three painters, and then, at my little murmur of interest, we graduated from the fine arts academy in Plovdiv, my husband and I, and now our son studies in Sofia, at the best school.

R. had stepped away as she spoke, turning his attention to the walls. She began to tell us about the paintings, glad to have an audience; she paused between sentences for me to translate, though I couldn't always follow what she said.

It was easy to tell apart the three artists as we scanned the walls: Her own paintings were swirling pale abstractions, her son's glossy female nudes. Her husband's work was larger and more striking, painted with the angular stylization of socialist-era art. Almost all of Sofia's public art was in this style, which I liked, more or less, though my Bulgarian friends pursed their lips at my admiration. *Mnogo sots*, they would say, very socialist, not just about murals and monuments but about music, too, about movies and books, dismissing at a stroke whole generations. The largest of the paintings in the main room formed a series, each of them featuring a central figure with a lyre, his neck bent toward it as if playing for himself alone. That's Orpheus, the woman said, do you know the story? I did, I had read Ovid in school, and when I said this her whole face lifted and lit up. How wonderful, she said, and then, he was from here, you know, he was Bulgarian, you can see his tomb in the south. I made a sound of polite interest, I had heard this before, and knew that for many people here the spiritual nation was still defined by its most expansive borders, *Bulgaria na tri moreta*, Bulgaria of the three seas, when for a brief moment it encompassed the whole of Thrace. I translated this too for R., and then, since he didn't know the story, I sketched it for him: the wedding and the snake, the descent, the trees that uprooted themselves to dance, and then (though this wasn't in the paintings) the Bacchantes, the slaughter, the head singing its way to Lesbos. We moved slowly, respectfully, through each of the rooms, and then, in the last, the woman directed us down a narrow staircase to a lower level. It was too steep for her, she said, not following us down, but take your time, look at whatever you like. The wooden planks made alarming noises as we descended, and I steadied myself against the wall; halfway down R. placed his hand on my shoulder, as if I were leading him through the dark. The basement was partitioned like the story above it, but it was unfinished; the floors were concrete, the space lit by bare bulbs hanging from wires. The walls here were crammed even more frantically with paintings, which were mounted haphazardly, wherever there was space, without any thought for coherence. In one room there was a heap of canvases stacked one on top of another, several columns of them piled almost to the ceiling, and I paused before them while R. explored the other rooms. This was where they put the paintings that didn't sell, I supposed; they were displayed upstairs for a while and then moved here to make room. There were hundreds of them, enough for a life's work, for several lives. It was a kind of trash heap, I thought, or might as well be; they would just sit there, gathering dust and mold, they would never be looked at again. They were buried here, along with the hours and days they had taken, the effort. We have an idea that the things we make will last, but they never do, or almost never; we make them and value them for a while and then they're cleared away. There's no metaphysics in it, I thought as I stood there staring at the heap of canvas and paint; it was like an automatic process, biological almost, a kind of excretion, there wasn't any meaning in it, it laid no claim upon the future. And of course I thought of the pages I number and stack like those paintings, the things I have made, how arduous and ardent the effort, I thought, though I might as well have been counting stones as pages, I might as well have been stacking grains of sand. I repeated the words to myself, ardor and arduous, struck as I had been before by the false similarity between them; I rolled them around without intention, it hardly counts as thought, until as if by their own engendering there appeared among or against them a new word, ordure, the three words linked and tumbling, consequence and cause, until R. came up behind me and placed his hand on my neck, pulling my face toward his own.

I drew away from him after a moment. Let's go, I said, taking his hand and pulling him toward the stairs; I wanted to escape the house and the weight of what filled it. When we climbed from the basement we found the woman waiting for us in the main room, standing hopefully at the glass table that served for a counter. There was a slight wilting in her frame when she saw we were empty-handed, something like a wave receding, though her smile never faltered as she asked whether we had enjoyed what we had seen. Oh yes, I said, very much, so many wonderful things, as if I were trying to make amends for the thoughts I had just had. It felt wrong to leave so quickly, having stayed so long, and I asked if she had a card, saying we would love to see the studio they kept in Sofia. She didn't, she said, but she took a sheet of paper from a drawer, on which she wrote in beautiful Cyrillic an address we promised to visit. She kept smiling as she handed this to me, but I could see she didn't believe what I had said; her gaze had gone a little unfocused, she was already staring past us at the empty street.

Outside, I wanted to tell R. why I had needed to leave so suddenly, but as I began to speak what I had felt seemed ridiculous, out of scale, and I let it drop. It was already late afternoon, and we angled our way back to the busier part of town. We didn't have any plans for the evening, and as we walked I kept an eye on the walls of the buildings beside the road, which were crowded with posters for concerts and exhibitions and plays, a surprising number for such a small town, I thought, posters mounted over other posters, bulging like plaster from the walls. Most of them were for small venues, clubs and cafés, but there was a series of performances held within the walls of the ruined fortress, too; the stage of ages, they called it, symphony and opera and ballet. We had been saving Tsarevets for the evening anyway; it would be brutal in the day, exposed to the sun and with almost no shade to be found. I saw that there was a concert that night, members of the Sofia Opera and Ballet performing *Lakmé*, the opera by Delibes. I had never seen it live, I told R., but it was the first opera I owned on CD, two discs I had played again and again. It was like a door opening onto my adolescence, I felt, a chance to share it with him, and suddenly it seemed important that we go, Please, I said, can we go, please, surprising us both with my insistence. He had never been to an opera before, but he was willing; it would be a new experience, he said, he was eager for new experiences.

We had a late lunch at a restaurant near the hotel. It was almost empty, there were only a few solitary men nursing beers, though the air was still heavy with smoke from the afternoon rush. The large windows along the back wall offered the same view as our room, and R. and I sat at a table next to one of them, looking out at the hills and their crowded houses. These had been grand once, I thought, they rose three or sometimes four stories high; the grandest were built at the very edge of the rock, their walls flush with the cliff. Most of the façades were white, and they gleamed where the sun struck them, their windows shuttered against the heat, but there were other colors too, the bright yellows and blues and reds of the National Revival. I'd be scared to live here, R. said, it looks like the houses could just slide down the hill. I hummed a reply and he laughed. You love it, don't you, he said, you always love sad places. Then he lifted himself up in his seat to look down the slope of our own hill, toward the banks of the river. Look, he said, and pointed to a series of shacks, what seemed almost like temporary shelters among the trees that filled the valley, with cinder block walls and roofs of corrugated metal. Do you think somebody lives there, he asked, and I said I did, I could see a garden and a tiny yard barely large enough for the mule it enclosed. Why would they need a horse, R. said, and then answered his own question, maybe that's where the gypsies live. He settled back into his seat, losing interest, but I kept looking at that little house shadowed by trees and in earshot of the river, where it must be cool, I thought, even on the hottest days. When I looked back at him R. was watching me, folding the edge of his napkin up and then pressing it back down. Are you sad, he said, and I shrugged, not sure if I was. I looked back to the window, not at the houses now but at the forested hills beyond Tsarevets, which looked almost pristine, except for one crest where large billboard letters spelled out TECHNOPOLIS, a chain of electronics stores. It's the only thing we can do, right, R. said, it's the only thing that makes sense. It was a conversation we had had many times in the past weeks, and since he knew what I thought I didn't respond. The waiter came then, anyway, bringing the pizza we had ordered. Don't you think so, R. continued once he had gone, and I hesitated before answering, looking down at the slice of pizza I had taken but not lifting it from the plate. I don't know, I said finally, I don't know if it's the right thing. And then, after a pause, But it's not the only thing, I said, you know that, you know you could stay, maybe we're giving up too fast. I would have said more but R. cut me off, he made the annoyed sound I expected, clucking his tongue. But we tried, he said, and I can't live here. I'd just sit all day by myself, waiting for you to come home, playing computer games, that's not a life, he said, we couldn't be happy like that. I started to say that he would make friends, that he could keep looking for a job; there were call centers where they needed European languages, with Portuguese and good English he could find something at one of them. Or he could take classes, I said, he could study again at the school in Studentski grad where he had spent a semester. You could stay, I said, you could make a life here, you wouldn't have to just sit at home. But I couldn't put much energy into what I said; he had made a decision, what was the point of talking. I love you, I said, we love each other, it should be enough, though even as I said this I knew it was unfair.

R. had been watching me, but at this he lowered his eyes. He brought his hand to his face and then bent his head forward, spreading his fingers as if to run them through his hair, which had been long until a few days before, when he buzzed it down to a centimeter or two. He rubbed his scalp a few times, and then dropped his hand back to the table. *Skupi*, he said, his tone imploring me for something, I don't know, what if we can't make it work once I leave, maybe this is my chance and I'm ruining it, he said, maybe I only have one chance to be happy. Am I doing the wrong thing, he said, looking at me, tell me what I should do. He met my eyes, and I felt that he really did want me to choose for him, that he would accept the decision I made; I can say yes to him, I thought, I can say yes, stay with me, I can grab hold of him. The words were on my tongue, I even took a breath to speak them, but I couldn't speak them, and I looked back down at my food. It would have violated something to say them, his freedom, I suppose, the choice he was so ready to hand over. You have to decide, I said finally, I can't tell you what to do.

He looked out the window, nodded, then turned back. Well, he said, we've already decided, right, we bought the ticket, it would be stupid to change our minds. Besides, he said, we're not giving up, we'll make it work, you'll come to Lisbon when you're on vacation, and there's the job fair in London this winter, you'll find something. I had been look-ing for a teaching job in a city where he would want to live, somewhere in the north, in a clean place, he had said, a coun-try where things worked like they should. But jobs were hard to come by, and it was hard for me to believe that R. would find in those countries, in any country, the life he thought he wanted. Though that wasn't the right way to put it, I thought, he didn't have a particular life in mind, something we could work for together; he acted as though life were something that would find him, in some city he had yet to see. Still, I pretended to be sure, as much for myself as for him, we would figure it out, I said, of course we would, we belonged with each other, I was his.

As we climbed the hill to the fortress after our meal I

could almost feel the centuries peeling back, exposing a world whose brutality was clear in the walls raised up to resist it. The way things are now, it's hard to imagine the country that could make this, R. said as we bought our tickets and began walking the long strip of stone leading to the fortress, pausing to stare at the huge square frame for gates that once would have barred our way. We weren't alone on the path up the hill; there were others too, couples mostly, some of them in clothes that made me feel underdressed, the women picking their way gingerly over the stony ground in heels. Apart from the occasional sign and a few wooden staircases granting access to the ruins, there was little to distract us as we walked the uneven ground, making our way around boulders and the ruins of walls. As we turned past one of these walls we surprised three men chatting, dressed in medieval costumes, two half-naked and muscular in leather tunics and a third in a kind of peasant cloth. They snatched the cigarettes from their mouths and stood up, one of the larger men unfurling his whip; and then, seeing our lack of interest, they leaned back against the stone, entirely contemporary in their strange clothes. At first I thought they might be from the opera, members of the chorus waiting for their call, but their costumes weren't right, and I realized they must have been performing in some tourist reenactment, Ottoman soldiers and a Bulgarian peasant. They resembled anyway the images in the books that had given me what idea I had of the history of the place, a set of slim illustrated volumes, comic books almost, a children's history of Bulgaria filled with barbaric invaders and mothers in tears, villains and victims stark in their frames. There were multiple versions of the story, I knew; in some the Bulgarians were valiant, in some savage and cruel, holding out for months against overwhelming forces, ceding an inch of ground at a time. There's no getting to the truth of such things, they're so far in the past, though nearly everyone I had met talked about the fall of Tsarevets in 1393 as if it were a personal grief. I hate the Turks, the woman who cuts my hair finds an occasion to say every time I sit in her chair; I'm sorry, but I can never forgive them, they are a terrible people.

We reached the top of the hill, where the medieval atmosphere was broken by two large trucks parked close to the ruins, each of them marked SOFIISKA NATSIONALNA OPERA I BALET in the block Cyrillic of government pronouncements. Tents had been set up to sell wine and refreshments, and genteel white folding chairs were arrayed on wooden platforms in front of the stage, where men in costumes, doubling as stagehands, were arranging scenery and props. A few potted plants and a painted backdrop sketched an idea of a forest, while complicated wooden scaffolding scaled the medieval wall, at the top of which a large statue of Ganesh reached out his many arms. I tried to take it in while R. flipped through the program: the ruins, the socialist-era trucks, the European refinement of the audience, the nineteenth-century sets, the ancient god serenely gazing; it was like a palimpsest with no original text, just endless layers peeling away, and I felt a quick shudder of vertigo, as though the ground might swing open beneath me.

I was surprised by how large an audience there was for a summer opera in a little town, and for an opera not quite in the standard repertoire. R. didn't know anything about it, of course, and as we waited for the performance to start, listening to the clatterings of the invisible orchestra, the occasional brass instrument clearing its throat, I gave him a sketch of the story, how a British soldier falls in love with a young priestess, who betrays her vows and then, when she's betrayed in turn, kills herself in a sacred grove. Well, that sounds awful, R. said. It's really not the best choice for a first opera, I said, wanting to lower his expectations, feeling protective of the experience I had been so eager to share. But I loved it when I was a kid, I said, and it has some beautiful music; though I worried that even the music would be less transporting than I remembered. And I was right, there was something a little embarrassing about it; everything seemed hopelessly dated, the sentimental music and oriental fantasy of a plot, and the first notes of the overture made clear that the performance wouldn't be very good. Bulgaria had a storied history in opera, it had produced some of the best singers I had listened to in my bedroom as a teenager, my hoarded recordings; but musicians too were fleeing westward, now that they could, leaving behind them anyone whose talents couldn't buy them a ticket out. It was a cruel thought, I was ashamed of it even as I cringed at the poorly tuned strings and splattered brass, the wooden movements of chorus and dancers. Most of the singers were past whatever prime they had had, though the oldest were the most impressive, I thought, an almost elderly bass and especially a mezzo whose voices, however they wobbled or frayed, had retained some ambered texture of accomplishment. I wondered if any recordings of their younger voices had survived; I could only guess, from the moments of resonance, the few ringing tones, at the mastery they had once possessed. That mastery must grow feebler by the day, I thought, it must be painful to feel it go. But it was Lakmé herself who mattered most, she had almost the only music in the opera worth hearing: the flower duet, which everyone knows and which has gone dull with repetition, and the bell song, when her father forces her to sing to the point of collapse, the music demanding the athleticism and suffering opera has always expected of its heroines. The soprano in the role was the only singer who was very young, in her twenties, a woman at the start of her career; she was a pleasure to watch, lovely and thin and with a pretty voice that was affectingly pure, maybe too untested for the role, so that the line between character and singer blurred and I was worried for her in the final bars of her big scene.

I remembered every note of the music, though I hadn't heard it for years. I must have been fourteen when I bought the CD, a London double set I picked out because of a single name, a soprano I knew my teacher adored, already I wanted to imitate him in everything. I remember falling asleep to the soldier's arias as sung by a tenor whose voice, which I've never found on another recording, was beautiful and light-bodied and pure, embodying my every ambition; as I listened to him I imagined the life my own voice would lead me to, scrubbed of shame. It didn't matter that the performance in Veliko Turnovo was poor; as I sat beside R. I felt that hope again. I was overcome by feeling for him, and it was painful not to touch him, even to reach my hand to his. Caution had become an instinct, and even here, if there wasn't actual danger I could imagine the discomfort any display of affection would cause. But we had our repertoire of covert gestures, the brushed elbow or knee, the slight pressure of a foot, and we made use of them as the night deepened and the air chilled and the ruins stood out more eerily in the lights. Looking at them I felt, with a force beyond the figures of my children's history, beyond any history at all, how ancient the place was; it was a battlefield we sat on, every inch of the ground had been steeped in blood, it must still be in the chemistry of the soil.

At the end of the opera, when the scattered bodies had risen for their applause, R. seemed less moved than bemused, looking at me as if to say is that all? The ovations were long and generous, especially for Lakmé, who left the stage half-interred by flowers. Then, before we could rise, an announcement was made that in twenty minutes the *spektakul zvuk i svetlina*, the sound and light show over Tsarevets, would begin. This was famous enough that R. had heard of it, and he wanted to go, even though it was cold now, the chill had deepened through the performance, and we were both tired after the day. I had been disappointed by the light show the year before, and I wasn't excited at the thought of sitting through it again; but it was short, fifteen minutes or so, and I resigned myself to it as we began to move with the crowd down the hill. There weren't any lights to guide us, except for the beams of one or two flashlights some members of the audience had known to bring. There was stumbling and cursing, but also a kind of good cheer, people were laughing and chatting, and in the dark I slipped my arm through R.'s, pressing him against me. I knew he had been disappointed by the opera, which hadn't brought about the closeness between us I had hoped for, and I felt in some obscure way that I had failed. A group of young people nudged us aside as they passed, raucous, singing melodies from the opera and swinging two-liter plastic bottles of beer: music students from the university, who seemed to know their way well enough in the dark.

I let go of R.'s arm as we reached the bottom of the hill, where lights met us again along the stone road, from which it was a five- or ten-minute walk to the observatory point where we would watch the show. Not many of the other operagoers joined us there, they scattered to their cars or set off on foot for home. The benches at the little plaza were full anyway, packed with children and what I took for their grandparents, the very old and the very young, as though everyone of vital age had been called away. R. and I stood behind the benches, watching the last well-dressed couples bend into their cars and slide off, until the speakers behind us popped awake and the lights in the square went out. R. made a humming noise of anticipation, and all of the bodies on the benches stiffened with attention. But as the music started, a kitsch fusion of folk instruments and Slavic chorus and dated synthesizer, as different quadrants of the hill and its ancient walls were illuminated, now in red, now blue and green, I felt myself receding from the square, from the light and sound. For hours I had managed not to think about R. leaving, about the uncertainty of our future, the guilt I felt no matter how I tried to dismiss it. I had never wanted permanence before, not really, or I had wanted my freedom more; I had accepted that passionate feeling faded, all my earlier experience had confirmed it, when love that seemed certain simply dissolved, on one side or both, for no particular reason, leaving little trace. But what I felt for R. was different, it didn't dissolve, and I wanted to believe in our language of boundlessness and the impossibility of change; to let it go would mean there had been bad faith, on one or both of our parts, maybe it isn't fair to think that but I thought it.

The lights were acting out some mounting drama, it was hard to say precisely what. The hill, which had at first been illuminated quadrant by quadrant, was now swept by red and blue lights, first in one direction and then the other. It must have meant the clashing of armies, though which were the virtuous Bulgarian forces and which the victorious Turks was lost on me, despite the narration of two children who stood on the rearmost bench, whispering excitedly to each other *Turtsite! Turtsite!* at each sweep of the lights. Whatever was happening a climax was approaching, it was clear in the martial lament of the music and also in the lights, which were mounting ever higher, toward the citadel itself and its reconstructed tower, though the effect was dampened by an anachronistic line of vehicles, the opera trucks at the fore, making its way down the hill. Then, from the tower, beams of light shot out, first in one direction, then in the other, then in both directions at once. What could it possibly mean, I wondered; it was clear it meant something, even the children were rapt, everyone sat transfigured. At the far end of one of the benches I saw that an old man had bent his head and covered his face with his hands, and that his shoulders were shaking as he wept. Then the lights went dark, and the speakers behind us fell silent, and from the hill itself in front of us rolled the slow sound, unamplified, of bells. There were many of them ringing together in the darkness, their tolling layered and fluid, the most affecting music of the evening, I thought, plangent and bare. And then, as they continued to ring, the hill was suddenly ablaze with light, not the colored floods of the warring sides but a white light, unsparing, so that every tree stood out and every stone was exposed, the ineffective walls, the whole much-repaired skeleton of it laid out at once grievous and proud. I heard R. make a little gasping sound beside me of marvel or dismay, and suddenly I was inside it, the wonder of the place, for a brief time at least I felt it too. Then the hill went dark again, and silent, and in the pause before anyone spoke or moved to leave I leaned toward R., wanting to feel him beside me, and for a moment he pressed warm against me in the dark.

III

HARBOR

Even in the dark I liked to look at it, though the sea was never truly dark, even now in the off-season it caught the light of the moon, which hung high and almost full, and of the few restaurants and hotels that were open in the new town, so that the whole harbor shimmered with points of light. It had been months since I had seen the sea, a year, and I was hungry for it; I had stepped to the edge of the terrace to check my phone but found myself staring at the sea instead. You could lose yourself in it, that was what drew me, it was beautiful but also it was like looking at nothing, the sight of it drowned out thinking like the sound of it drowned out noise, and at first I didn't hear the others calling me to join them. I smiled as I turned, though I resented being called back, and saw that they were standing in a circle beside the tables where they had been smoking and talking, their glasses empty. Come here, one of the American writers said, we're playing spin the bottle, and I laughed and took my place. We were choosing partners; there would be a reading to close the

festival at the end of the week, and we would read in pairs,
one American, one Bulgarian. A Bulgarian writer held one of
the wine bottles we had emptied; he crouched in the center of
the circle and then stepped back to the periphery once he had
set it spinning, which it did crazily over the cobblestones of
the patio. He was the oldest of us, midfifties and handsome,
a champion boxer when he was young and now a coach of
some sort. All the Bulgarians had other careers, there's no
such thing as a professional writer in Bulgaria, and no writing
programs, either, or almost none; they worked in business, or
as journalists, one ran a satirical website all my students loved,
one was a priest. And they had all published books, some of
them several, so that though the program was for emerg-
ing writers it was hard to tell the difference between them
and the writers still inside the restaurant, the famous writers. That wasn't true for the Americans, who were younger
and less accomplished; most were still in graduate programs
for writing, or had just finished. We were boring in compari-
son to them, I thought as the bottle came to a stop and, to a
chorus of cheers, the boxer stepped forward and shook the
hand of one of the Americans. There was something a little
sheepish about the pair of them, maybe the erotic overtones
of the game caused them to lean away from each other as they
shook hands, each staying decidedly in his own sphere. N.,
who ran the website, took the bottle next. He was a bigger
man, not quite fat, not quite handsome, the friendliest and
funniest in the group; he had made us laugh to tears over dinner and he made us laugh now, when he took his American
partner by the shoulders and hugged him close, he was so

happy, they would be brothers forever, a toast, he said, taking him to the table and its bottle of rakia.

There were six of us left, we tightened our circle as another Bulgarian writer, the only woman in their cohort, took the bottle and spun it on the cobblestones. But before it could come to a stop a voice called out in Bulgarian and then a waitress from inside stepped in between us, wagging her finger and snatching the bottle up from the ground. *Chakaite*, one of the Bulgarians said, hold on, we're almost finished, but the waitress said *Ne, ne mozhe*, it's not permitted, we were being too loud, people lived above the restaurant, and the bottle, what if it broke, what a mess, and then she turned and walked back inside, the bottle cradled against her chest. We looked at one another, embarrassed, and then the Bulgarian woman shrugged and turned back to the table. Most of the others joined her, one or two went inside the restaurant, where the writers who taught the workshops were sitting, one Bulgarian and one American, we had had our first sessions earlier that day. I stepped away again, not wanting to join them, I pulled my phone out but put it back in my pocket unchecked. I can't, R. had said, wiping his face, I don't think I can, I don't know what I feel, I have to figure out my life. He was sitting cross-legged on his bed, his computer open in front of him, he kept leaning toward the screen and back. But Skups, I said, using my name for him, our name for each other, that's what we've been doing, we're figuring out our lives, you are my life, I didn't say, but I thought it, for two years he had been my life. Every couple of months I flew to Lisbon to spend a long weekend with him, a week, whenever I had a break I stayed in his tiny student's room, we slept together in the narrow bed he was sitting on now. I'm trying, I said to him, I'm applying for jobs, but there were no jobs, or none I could get, it was too expensive to hire Americans, they said, especially with the crisis, if I had an EU passport it would be different. It's impossible, R. said, you know it's impossible, we have to accept it, I have to live my life. I had to live my life too, and I wanted a different life, not a life without R. but a life in a new place, I couldn't keep living the same day again and again, the hours of teaching, I wanted a new life too.

On the patio a plan was forming to leave the restaurant and explore the town. It was a warm night, early June, still a week or two before the shops would open for the summer tourists, with signs in Russian hung out over cheap souvenirs; we would have the streets to ourselves. N. made a quick trip inside the restaurant, to the long table where food had been laid out, and returned with a bottle of wine, which he held low and tight against his body, hiding it from the waitress. Rations, he said, very important. The restaurant was near the hotel, at the tip of the little peninsula that formed the southern side of the harbor, and the street we walked along was like all the others in the old town, cobbled and lined on both sides with unpainted wooden houses in the National Revival style, two- or three-story buildings, oddly off-kilter and asymmetrical, with elaborate wooden beams buttressing upper floors jutting out over the foundations. They were in varying stages of upkeep, some renovated, others barely shacks, even here along the most desirable streets near the shore, where buildings jostled for a glimpse of the sea. Most of them were empty, shuttered hotels and vacation homes, but occasionally the sound of a television reached us from inside, or light spilled through the slats of the wooden shutters, a few people lived here all year long. I was walking with another American, a graduate student in a program he hated in the South. He was younger than I was, and fit; in the mornings he ran along the sea, on the path that led to the new town, where the shops were open, he said, it was a real city, not just a museum. He was friendly and I tried to match his friendliness, it was why I was here, I told myself, to meet people, to make friends. But I didn't trust myself, I was too eager, I caught myself looking at him, at almost every man I passed, with a kind of hunger R. had shielded me from, I mean the thought of R. It might be possible, I thought about the other writer, he looked at me sometimes in a way that made me think maybe I could have him, or he could have me, we could have a little romance, though that wasn't what I wanted; I wanted something brutal, which was what frightened me, I wanted to go back to what R. had lifted me out of. It was a childish feeling, maybe, I wanted to ruin what he had made, what he had made me, I mean, the person he had made me.

We were trailing behind the others, we could hear them ahead of us in the dark, their occasional bursts of laughter. We were walking up Apolonia, the main thoroughfare, though it wasn't until we reached the center of town that there were any real signs of life, some open shops, a restaurant, a man at a table outside, hunched over a slice of pizza. We caught up with the others in front of a convenience store, and waited until N. and the priest emerged with new bottles of wine and a stack of plastic cups. N. handed these out as the priest busied himself with one of the bottles, cutting the foil at the neck with a pocketknife attached to his keys, working at it slowly, with the deliberateness of drunkenness. He had arrived after the rest of us, driving in from Veliko Turnovo. We had all been curious to meet him, but there was nothing especially priestly about the man who appeared dressed all in black, not in a cassock but in jeans and a T-shirt he wore tucked in, tight on his thin frame. He had a young man's beard, scraggly and unkempt, a sign of laziness more than devotion, I might have thought. Only his hands marked him out, the fingers long and thin, a scholar's hands, with the weird sliding grace of someone accustomed to ritual. Or maybe I had this impression because of the way I had seen him raise his hand to a man's lips earlier in the evening, when the distinguished Bulgarian writer, elderly and reclusive, asked for a blessing before he read. He had become priestly in that moment, he had stood solemnly while the writer pressed his lips to the third joint of the second finger of his right hand, and then he made the sign of the cross over the writer's bowed head. It had surprised me, it was a gesture I hadn't seen in years, not made in earnest, not since the year I had played at conversion in graduate school, when I had made it myself or had it made over me at the rail of a church in Boston, where I stood with my arms crossed over my chest, my mouth sealed by my disordered life, as I thought of it then.

There was nothing solemn about the priest now. Once he had opened the bottle he made a direct line for D., the youngest American, who from the first had been the object of greatest interest for the Bulgarian men. This was especially true of the priest, whose attentions had gone quickly from charming to comic and then, as they persisted, become disquieting. For most beautiful first, he said, pouring wine into her cup, his English almost nonexistent, and she smiled and looked away, cringing a little. He came around to each of us then, gallant as he filled our cups, though he refused to meet my gaze, as he had all day, my attempts to speak with him defeated by the odd way he spoke Bulgarian, very fast and with a tripping enunciation that made him impossible for me to understand. It was the accent of his region, one of the other Bulgarians said to me, *selski aksent*, a village accent. But it wasn't his accent that made him distant with me, I thought, though maybe it was uncharitable of me to assume he shared the views of his colleagues, or some of his colleagues, like the priest who had called, the previous summer, for all decent people to line the route of the Pride parade and throw stones at the queers.

I took advantage of the pause to check my phone again. We were taking a break, that was how R. had left things, but though I tried not to think it I knew the break was final. For the past two weeks we hadn't had any contact, stopping our Skype chats and emails, which had become essential to the structure of my day, even as they had also begun to seem like a trap, taking me away from writing, keeping me up too late. He never wanted to hang up, I'll be so bored, he would say, I'll be so lonely, and the next day I would struggle to make it through class. They had come to feel like a trap but without them I found the evenings intolerable, there was too much time for thinking, too much time for remorse. It wasn't really true that we had no contact, we still looked at each other's Facebook pages; the night before I had posted photos of the drive from Sofia to Sozopol, of our group beside the sea, probably that was what had spurred him to send, very early that morning, the message I had worried over all day. It was full of regret and self-recrimination, I've broken the best thing, he wrote, he didn't know why he had done it, it was just the same thing again and again, he said, it's like I hate my own happiness, which was a phrase I had repeated to myself all day. This had been the worst part about distance, the helplessness I felt when he was anxious or sad, as he often was, when nothing I could say would comfort him. Sex could comfort him, or just the presence of my body beside his, he wanted physical comfort, and it was terrible to think of him in his room alone. I know I can't fix it, he said, I know it's too late, we can't go back, he spoke of it as if it were the distant past, and this made me angry, since what was the point of his message then, why had he sent it to me, why had he drawn me back to him, drawn me back but only so far.

The priest had finished making his rounds, he had emptied one bottle and carried another that was half full, which he lifted to his mouth and drank from deeply, thirstily. He started singing as we walked on, following the road as it opened up, past the houses of the old town, into a kind of plaza beyond which a tree-lined avenue led up to the highway. I couldn't understand the words of his song but the melody was familiar, and after a moment I realized it was the anthem of one of the football teams, I had heard groups of men singing it in the streets, Bulgarian flags draped across their shoulders. No one else took it up now, though he didn't seem bothered, he walked ahead singing, swinging the wine bottle to punctuate his phrases.

N. stepped onto a bench at the edge of the plaza, trying to get our attention. *Dami i gospoda*, he said, repeating it in English, ladies and gentlemen, and we gathered around him, except for the priest, who kept walking into the darkness, singing his song, until the Bulgarian woman ran to catch him by the shoulder and turned him back to us. Oh, he said, dipping his head in apology, and then he took a place at the back of the group, his hands crossed at his waist, holding the bottle low, an image of meekness. Ladies and gentlemen, N. said again, spreading his arms wide like a politician and making all of us laugh. He was from Burgas, a city some twenty or so kilometers away, and of all the Bulgarians he knew Sozopol best. I worked as a tour guide here when I was young, he said, and now I would like to tell you, American friends, a few things about my country. This is the most old town in Bulgaria, he said, its name is Greek, it means—and here he paused, groping—*spasenie*, at which a couple of the Bulgarians said salvation, which he repeated, nodding, salvation. Once this was Greek, there are still many Greeks here, they build many little churches we still have, and it was true, everywhere you looked there were tiny chapels, places to pray for fishermen out at sea. There was one of these across from our hotel, facing the water, and I had entered it very early that morning, as I set off to stroll through the town on my own. It had been restored, every inch of the walls had been covered in bright blues and golds, portraits of the Virgin, the saints, and on the ceiling a large, intricate painting of the sun, multiple spoked disks laid atop one another like a complicated set of gears. The remnants of candles stuck up from trays filled with sand in front of the image of the Virgin; a pile of these candles, very long and thin, sat next to a donation box at the door. There's a feeling such places accrue, a residue of use, and I considered taking one of those candles and saying a prayer of my own, something to do with R. maybe, that he be happy, that we both be happy, together or apart. Now, in the plaza, as N. continued to speak I looked at the priest, who stood quietly, still calm, his hands crossed at the waist, the bottle dangling, his head slightly bowed. He could almost have been praying himself, though he wasn't praying, he was drunk, or maybe he was praying too, I don't know. It was a posture—the bowed head, the apparent meekness—I remembered from the man I had gotten to know that year in Boston, the priest in whose office I had sat nearly every week; it was the posture with which he met my zeal or desire for zeal, which seemed to bemuse him, as if he found it both sincere and unreal, which it was. I don't recognize the person I was then, when I read my journal from that time, or the handful of poems I wrote. I wanted to unmake myself, it seems to me now, I wanted to fit my life into a system that would deform it so entirely it would be unrecognizable.

But now N. interrupted his lecture, saying here he was, telling us about the town, it was hard work, and he was a professional, he shouldn't work for free. I want money, he said, making us laugh, American money, does someone have a quarter, and someone did, it was fished out of a pocket and handed over. George Washington, he cried, a sudden change of tone, I love George Washington, he is my favorite person. We laughed again and he looked up, Why are you laughing, he asked, which made us laugh more. Look, he said, holding up the coin, it says here Liberty, it is the most beautiful thing, most beautiful word, it is for this I love George Washington. He fights for freedom, like us, Bulgarians fight for freedom too. For five hundred years we are slaves to the Turks, but now we are free. It is the most important thing, Liberty. Hear hear! someone said, an American, and we all raised our cups to N., though most of them were empty already. He seemed pleased by this, he gave a quick bow, at which our toast turned more raucous, *Nazdrave*, we cried, the Bulgarian toast, *Nazdrave*. He hopped down from his perch, motioning us to be quiet, We are not drunk Romanians, he said. Then he held the quarter up, looking at it anew, and with a tone of real wonder asked What do I do with this money, which set us laughing again. Keep it, D. said, from the back of our circle where the priest stood too close to her, it means someone in America loves you. Ah, said N., beaming at her, pleased beyond words, and he slid the coin into his breast pocket and cupped his hands over it. I keep it forever, he said.

Then the priest said something I didn't catch, pointing with his bottle, and N. said Yes! The beach! I take you there, and we followed him across the square. I was eager to be festive with these people, to distract myself from the grief I had felt since receiving R.'s message, my own grief and grief at the thought of him alone in his room in Lisbon—though I didn't know where he was, of course, he had sent his message hours before and might already have recovered from his spasm of regret, who could know. I hung back a bit, as we reached the other side of the square, to look at the structure we were passing through, something like a covered patio between two buildings, while the others were descending the wooden staircase to the sea. There was a set of wooden counters, what looked like a sizeable bar, but all of it was abandoned now, strewn with trash and empty bottles. It must come alive in the season, I thought, though there was a kind of finality to its disuse, it was difficult to imagine that in a few weeks it would be transformed, packed with young people. I felt uneasy, and suddenly I realized I wasn't alone; a man, who must have been watching us as we passed, was leaning against the wall. He took a long drag from a cigarette, the tip flaring red in the dark, and met my eyes briefly before lowering his gaze. I almost thought he was there to cruise, that maybe this was a place men used, but he had an air of belonging, leaning against the wall, and I decided he must be something like a guard, keeping an eye on the place until it came to life again for the summer. Maybe he would stand there all night, I thought, but I didn't see any television or radio to keep him company, anything at all, there was nothing but the sea to mark the time. Or maybe there was an office or booth he would retreat to once we had passed, maybe he had only emerged on hearing our approach. I nodded to him as I moved toward the stairs, murmuring *Dobur vecher*, but he just raised his eyes again and flicked his spent cigarette to the ground.

There was a wooden platform at the bottom of the stairs, beside which the others had piled their shoes. I could see the whole coast, stretching from the old town, where we had eaten, which was quiet and dark, to the new town with its high-rise hotels, their windows facing the sea. One restaurant was still open, brightly lit in red and blue, and I could hear music, Balkan pop, the uneven drums and pipes, a woman's voice singing restlessly around them. I couldn't make out the words but they were always the same: something about love, I thought, something about loss. The beach was artificial, someone had told us, they trucked tons of sand in to this particular cove; the rest of the coast was rocky, there was nowhere to bathe, though young men, despite the posted warnings, climbed the rock walls each summer to jump into the sea. The Roman wall along the old town was perpetually lit by floodlights bolted to the rocks beneath it. I had walked beside it earlier that day, with a friend who had traveled from Burgas so we could spend an hour or two together, and he had shown me where the original wall ended and modern reconstruction began, a thin strip of metal running between them. Only the lowest stones were ancient, and I knelt to lay my hands on them, jagged and pocked from the salt air, imagining the hands that, generations ago, had placed them there. This city had been a major port once, the Romans had dedicated it to Apollo, setting a great statue of the god like a guard against the sea, though the statue had disappeared long ago.

From where I stood now I could see the path we had taken, my friend and I, and I remembered too how he had pointed to this beach, telling me that in summer very late at night you could find men here, that there were sheltered places in the rocks where you could go with them. I wondered if I would want that now, if there were men to be had. Shortly after R. had told me he wanted to end things I had gone to the city center, seeking I don't know what. For almost two years I had been with no one but R., and for the past three months I hadn't been with anyone at all; I went out in search of feeling, I suppose, or maybe the absence of feeling. I descended the flights of stairs to the bathrooms at the National Palace of Culture, though for so long I imagined I had left them behind, that I had been lifted out of them, as I was in the habit of putting it to myself, into a new life. I had thought that before, when I sat in that room in Boston with the priest, I had thought in precisely those terms, I am being lifted out of it, not by my own agency but by some intervening force: God, love, *edno i sushto*, one and the same. But we are never lifted out of such places, I think now, and so I went back to the bathrooms beneath NDK, I had never stopped thinking about them; even as I lay with R., flooded with love, there was a part of me untouched by him, a part that longed to be back here. My hands shook as I undid my belt at the urinals, out of excitement or dread, I felt I could hardly breathe. Almost immediately a man stepped up next to me, nineteen or twenty perhaps, very beautiful, his large cock already hard. Possibly he was a hustler, he was so eager, though he didn't make any demands as I reached over and took him in my hand, feeling the thick warmth of him as I closed my eyes and inhaled deeply, trying to discern what I wanted, knowing how easy it would be to take him into the neighboring room with its stalls. I heard him whisper *Iskash li*, do you want it, and though I did want it I let him go, I hid away my own hardness and fled.

It was a beautiful night, the nearly full moon casting its light upon the water, and I wanted to be with them now, these people I hardly knew who seemed so at ease with one another. I took off my shoes and walked up to N., our erstwhile

guide, who was smoking a cigarette, standing well away from
the surf where the others were wading, letting the waves
brush their ankles and calves, shouting and laughing. Hi, he
said, smiling at me, speaking in English though my Bulgarian was better, it is beautiful here, no? And I said it was, very
much so, *prekrasno*. He asked me about the morning's work-
shop, and I told him it was fine, that they were interesting
writers, I liked them very much. And how was the Bulgarian
group, I asked, and he turned to me, smiling widely, and said
Today we talked about the G-spot of the story, how it is like
with a woman, it is difficult to make the story come. Ah, I
said, taken aback, I see. And then, after a pause, But I don't
understand, I said, why should the story be a woman? It was
a fair question, I thought, but he looked at me with blank
incomprehension, even though I had spoken in his language.
Couldn't it be a man, I asked, would it change anything, and I
thought he was going to say something in response, but then
our attention was claimed by a commotion farther down the
beach. What's that, I said as we started walking toward the
others, who had gathered in a circle, what's going on, and
then, as we heard whistles and catcalls and voices chanting
strip, strip, N. told me that the priest had said he wanted
to swim. We could see him now, already bare-chested, his
bearded face bright in the light of cell phone cameras brought
out of pockets. Immediately, catching sight of him, I felt myself in that strange state of vibrancy and stasis, like a flame
submerged in glass, sealed off as always when I feel desire I
shouldn't feel. Not that he was so desirable: he was thin and
pale, with a silver cross glinting on his chest. His hand drifted
to his jeans and he paused, letting the encouragement rise,

looking around the circle until he found D., eager as the rest, hooting and calling Take it off, and with a look that seemed to dedicate the act to her, the whole evening, the night and the sea, he undid the buttons of his fly and stripped. There was an eruption of cheers, and he began playing to the crowd, lifting his arms and flexing, smiling at the flashing lights; he was entirely one with them now, I thought, all his sanctity was gone. He wasn't naked, he was still wearing a pair of tight black briefs, and I was surprised to see they were a designer brand, sleek and European, not at all what I would have expected. He posed for a moment, balanced on his skinny legs, and then he turned his back to us and ran for the water, splashing at first awkwardly and then diving in, fully submerged. Jesus, I said to no one in particular, it must be so cold. He's crazy, N. said beside me, and then, three weeks ago he is in Israel, the Holy Land, and he swims in the river Jordan. It is forbidden to swim, but he doesn't care, he swims anyway. We watched him for a while before most of the group lost interest, turning to other pursuits, pouring the last of the wine. D. and the Bulgarian woman climbed the tall lifeguard's platform together, waving to us below. But I kept watching him, visible in the moonlight; he was a good swimmer, he seemed at home in the water, I thought, like a creature reconciled to what it was. I kept waiting for him to turn, to swim back, but he didn't, and finally in the dark I could hardly make him out at all. He's kind of far, isn't he, I said aloud, again to no one in particular, shouldn't he be turning around, and then N., who hadn't been paying attention, said Idiot, it's dangerous at night, and both of us shouted for him to come back. He didn't hear us at first, he kept swimming, and then the others were shouting too, in English and Bulgarian, and all of us were waving our arms. He stopped finally, and waved one of his own arms in response, and then he began swimming toward shore, more slowly, I thought, as though there were some force pulling back at him, some element working to bear him out farther still.

THE LITTLE SAINT

His name meant light, or that was the root of it, the root too of the word for holy, for any number of words associated with sanctity and the church; and this was why later, when I grew fond of him, I called him *Svetcheto*, the little saint. It made him laugh, both because it was bad Bulgarian, he told me, no one who actually spoke the language would say it, and also because he liked it, I thought, not the name but that I had made it up for him. I liked it too, not least because it was so at odds with the things we did together, with how I used him or how we used each other. And maybe there actually was something saintly about him, his slightness and quiet in the hoodie that framed his face like a monk's cowl when I saw him that first time, or in the bathrobe he wrapped around himself later, when I came to his door; and maybe there was something saintly in his endurance, too, I guess I think there was, in his desire for pain.

But that first day I didn't know his name, I thought probably I would never see him again. We had chatted online for the first time just an hour or so earlier, though I had looked at his profile often; he was always online, for months I had been fascinated by him. It was a kind of profile common enough in the States or Western Europe but I had never seen one like it here; it claimed that anyone who wanted to could fuck him, that he wanted it rough, that his only demand was to be fucked bare, he wanted as many loads as he could get. No limits whore, it said, in good pornographic English, with a Bulgarian translation beneath. I was curious to know what that meant here, no limits, and where he had learned it. Many of the things he listed were things I wanted, too, what I liked to be done to me, which is why I took so long to write him; we wanted the same things and so were incompatible, as people say. Maybe I came to be excited by the thought of doing to him what others had done to me, what in those weeks or months I had wanted done more often and to greater extremes. Maybe it happened slowly but it seemed sudden, the desire I felt for the boy whose photos appeared in little boxes that accompanied his profile, in one his face twisted in an erotic grimace, in another three fingers, his own, inserted in his ass.

The photos didn't give any real sense of him, I was surprised by how beautiful he was when he pushed back the hood he had raised against the rain, which was just a light rain, a relief from the early summer warmth. He was short and dark-skinned, with close-cropped black hair, and as he looked up at me I realized it was his eyes that made him beautiful; they were large and almond-shaped, a shade of grayish green. I was sheltering beneath the awning of the café where he had told me to wait for him, in a part of Mladost where it was impossible to find your way, he said; you had to have lived there a long time to make sense of the jungle of buildings, the warren of unnamed streets. It wasn't far from the apartment on campus where I lived, but it was on the other side of Malinov Boulevard, and there was little reason to explore beyond the supermarket where the whole neighborhood did its shopping. It was a Saturday, the café was full of couples and children. We acknowledged each other with a nod, and then I reached out to shake his hand as he looked away shyly, making me feel I had embarrassed him, that I had acted in some way I shouldn't. We murmured a greeting but didn't otherwise speak, he just turned and began to walk, leaving me to follow.

His building wasn't far, but he was right, it would have been difficult to find. There had been a plan here once, in Communist times, the huge *blokove* erected at intervals to leave green spaces between, parks and playgrounds, the remnants of which we passed through now. But any sense of order had been lost, the parks had been paved over, new buildings had sprung up in every empty space. Cars were parked on sidewalks, in the little alleys between buildings, on both sides of the road; drivers had to thread their way through the streets single file, cells in a clogged artery. He walked ahead, not speaking or looking back, moving quickly because of the rain, though maybe it was eagerness too, I thought, maybe he felt the excitement I felt, the blood rushing to my groin. I'll use you hard, I had written, after he told me what he wanted, get ready, I'll make you take it. It isn't easy to find men who will say that, the idea of it frightens them or turns them off; when finally I found someone to say it to me there was excitement but also gratitude and relief, maybe he was feeling that. Even in his hoodie it was clear how slim he was, he kept his hands in the pockets at the front and pulled the fabric tight around him, showing off his frame, and he wore tight jeans that advertised his legs and ass, which I found myself watching as we walked. It was the only condition I had set, that I didn't want to come in his ass; I want to shoot in your mouth, I had said, in your mouth and on your face. Really I wasn't sure I wanted to fuck him at all, I worried about disease, and the longer I fucked him the more danger there would be. Danger for him, too; I got tested every six months but I wasn't always careful, I wasn't fanatically safe. On his profile he had chosen the third option, not negative or positive but don't know, and in the text he had said he didn't care about status, anyone was welcome, he didn't want to know. People always lie, he would say to me later, why bother to ask, why should I believe them, why should I care.

His apartment was on the ground floor of a poorly maintained building, ten or twelve stories of discolored concrete, the façade run through with cracks. The door was a thick metal slab, meant for security, though it wasn't locked, wasn't even latched; he opened it by gripping it with both hands and pulling hard as it dragged. He left it open behind us; he would tell me later that the old women in the building couldn't open it on their own, if it was closed they would call out or rap on windows for someone to let them in. On my window, he complained, since his was the second apartment in the long hallway on the ground floor I followed him into, it's fucking annoying. His own space was more effectively guarded by the series of locks he undid, and by the bars that latticed the narrow window, which I glimpsed before he drew a curtain across it. We stood in the larger of two rooms, which had a TV and, facing it, a couch, between them a low table with an open laptop, an overflowing ashtray; the second room was to the right, with a narrow bed visible through the open door. There was another bed, or kind of bed, behind me, against the wall by the front door, a thin pallet laid over a long wooden chest or cupboard of some kind, an improvised frame. It was unmade, the sheets balled up at one end. This was where he slept; the apartment was his sister's, he didn't really live there. He was just visiting Sofia, though he had stayed for a long time, he said, and had no plans to leave.

I didn't know whether I should sit or lie on this bed, I stood waiting for a signal. He looked at me, hesitating, and then stepped forward. Neither of us spoke. I watched him, unsure how to begin, though I knew I should be the first to act. He smiled a little, as if he saw my uncertainty and forgave it, forgave it or mocked it, I'm not sure which. I knew the kind of disdain I had felt for men who weren't sure what they wanted, you could sense it from the first moment, the first tepid move; I had despised them sometimes for offering less than they had promised. He raised his hand and placed it on my chest, a tender gesture, and then he leaned toward me to kiss me. But I didn't let him kiss me, I would kiss him later but it wasn't the right way to begin, I grabbed his throat to stop him. He had closed his eyes but they opened now in surprise, and I held his gaze as I tightened my grip, not much, not to hurt him or frighten him but to assert something, to chastise him a little for having made the first move, though he had had to, we both knew, it had given me permission to begin. There was a kind of negotiation as we looked at each other, a question, and then he moaned low in his throat and closed his eyes again, and I knew that it would work between us. I turned his head a little, tilting it first to the left and then the right, as if I were examining him, but really I was examining myself, my willingness to master him as much as his willingness to be mastered. And then I pushed him away and dropped my hand and told him brusquely to get undressed.

He took another step back and lifted his hand to the zipper of his hoodie, which he drew down slowly, glancing at me and then looking away, seductive or shy. His chest was boyish, slender and almost hairless, his nipples small and dark and already tight with excitement. He was slow with his belt, too, and with the zipper of his jeans, not quite performing for me as he undid them and pushed his jeans and his briefs down to reveal his cock, which was already hard and sprang out, eager and comic. He posed for a moment, showing it off. It was thickish and hooded, the long foreskin even though he was hard drawn over the head. He pulled it back now, stroking himself two or three times before I told him to stop and he dropped his hand. I had spoken sternly, but I was glad to see it, that he was so eager, that he was enjoying himself. I wouldn't touch it, it was part of my role almost to pretend it wasn't there; I want to be a hole, he had typed in our chat, I want to be nothing but a hole. It was important to seem like I didn't care about his pleasure but I did care about it, very much, I wanted him to be hard. I took a step toward him, claiming ground and coming too close; I could feel his heat through the fabric of my shirt. We looked at each other, and before he dropped his eyes I felt an upwelling of tenderness for him. I wanted to kiss him, to be in a different kind of scene with him, but of course I couldn't change the scene, it would have been a breach of our contract. If it had been my usual role to dominate, to be cruel, to be cruel in that way, my role or my nature, I would have simply acted on my in-clination, I think; at least that's what I imagine it must be to act as the men I long for act, to want something and not ques-tion it. But I didn't kiss him, instead I ran my hands across his torso, the back of my hands, stopping when I reached his nipples, which I brushed across lightly several times, feeling them tighten further. Then I took them between my thumb and forefinger, gently at first, rubbing the tip in little circles, like a bullet, not twisting but massaging, so that he hummed slightly to show me that he liked it, and slowly I began to grip him harder, listening as his humming became more glot-tal and higher in pitch, became a whine. And then I grabbed him very hard, pinching and twisting in a way meant to hurt. He opened his mouth, not whining but gasping a single sylla-ble, Ah, his eyes clenched shut. But he didn't move his hands, which was the test, he didn't lift them to shield himself or loosen my grip, when I looked they were pressed against his thighs, fingers extended, the tips digging into his flesh. Good boy, I thought, though I didn't say it out loud. It became a kind of contest then, I wanted to make him ask me to stop. But he took what I gave him, when I pulled on them hard he even leaned back to stay upright, though that could only have increased his pain. I wouldn't find his limit, then, or not that way, and I acknowledged this by changing the direc-tion of my pulling, tugging him by his nipples not toward me but down. He resisted this at first, too, straining against me to maintain his position, not realizing until I yanked harder what I wanted him to do. And then he dropped to his knees.

I let go of him once I felt him begin to fall, I stayed upright, my hands at my sides. He had fallen hard, even with the rug we stood on it must have hurt. He leaned forward slightly, he bowed until his forehead almost touched me, he kept just the slightest space between us. I looked down at the crown of his head, the neatly cut hair spiraling out counterclockwise from the center, and I saw that without being told he had clasped his hands behind his back. Again I wondered where he had learned it, whether someone had taught him these gestures and codes, whether he had learned them himself online. I wondered if they made a coherent pattern, a kind of life, consistent, something like virtue, really, or were just a sort of ornament, a dream to be dipped into from time to time. But I didn't wonder this long; I was hard, I wanted more, and so I leaned forward just slightly, little more than a breath, letting my crotch brush his forehead. Immediately he lifted his face, he pressed his nose into me, breathing in hard, smelling me, and then he started rubbing his face against me, against my balls and then along the shaft of my cock where it was trapped by my jeans, rubbing first his forehead and then the side of his face and then his mouth and nose, up again to his eyes and forehead, making a circular movement that brought his whole face in contact with me. I had done this too, many times, it was a kind of animal instinct, the pleasure not of marking one's territory but of being marked; it was the pleasure of belonging to someone, I suppose, the pleasure of knowing one's place. On his face was a look of need and provocation, begging me for something or daring me, both, I think, he was leading me where he wanted.

I stood and watched him, enjoying not giving him what he wanted, though that isn't quite true, the not-giving was part of what he wanted; and part of what I wanted was this, to see him desire or perform desire, more intensely now as he started rooting into me, almost making me flinch. At first I couldn't understand what he was doing, he was moving his head back and forth just slightly, and then I realized he was trying to flip back the flap covering the zipper of my jeans. Once he had managed this, folding the fabric back with his nose, he rubbed his face against the metal, up and down, as if he were trying to undo it that way, all the while with his hands clasped behind his back. He wasn't trying to undo it, of course, this was part of his performance, but he was rubbing hard and fast enough that I thought it must be something else, too, a desire for pain, or if not pain then sensation of a particular sort, a kind of intensity. Take it out, I said finally. He looked up at me, smiling, and then brought his hands to my belt, slowly now, the urgency gone, and pulled the leather strap free of its buckle. He surprised me by removing the belt altogether, taking a moment to coil it around his hand before setting it ceremoniously beside him. There was something ceremonious about all of his movements, if they had been animal before they were exaggeratedly refined now, careful and precise. He pulled my jeans down, waiting for me to step out of them before he folded them and placed them beside the belt and the shoes I had kicked off. Only then did he bring his hands back to my waist and pull my underwear down, stretching the elastic to let my cock spring out, bobbing in the air as I lifted first one foot and then the other to let him pull the fabric free. He took my underwear in both his hands, spreading it across his open palms, and then buried his face in it, taking famished breaths, wanting whatever chemical traces I had left there, some mix of sweat and urine, of detergent and soap. His hands were covering his eyes but I almost rolled my own back in sympathy, I had felt the rush of it many times, that scent, but I had never watched someone else be overcome by it, I had never before been the cause of it. He folded them carefully and settled back on his knees before me.

He linked his hands behind his back again but almost immediately reached up to cup my balls in one hand, the first time he had actually touched me, my bare skin; I drew my breath in through my teeth at the shock, which was neither pleasure nor pain, but sensation, pure and unmarked. With his other hand he gripped the shaft and moved it to the right and left, up and down, not erotically, but as if examining it, I thought, like a physician; and maybe he *was* examining it, in part, looking for signs of disease though he claimed not to care about disease, I don't know. My first American cock, he said then, looking up at me and smiling, my first cut cock; his English was remarkable, he spoke flawlessly the language of hook-up sites and porn. He gripped more tightly as he pulled up the shaft, milking me, and at the tip there appeared a small drop, opalescent, almost clear. I should have stopped him as he leaned forward, I was giving him too free a rein, but I let him touch the tip of his tongue to the drop, not gathering it up but tasting it, and then he pulled back, so that it stretched out gossamer between us. He closed his eyes, his tongue still extended, and I felt again that he was acting something out, that he had slipped into a fantasy that had very little, had possibly nothing, to do with me. He was posing, inhabiting a scene, something out of porn, some image in which he was a star. He made these images, he would tell me later, they were his main source of income, he performed on webcam sites for men who paid him to do whatever they wanted. I love it, he said, all those guys watching me and jerking off, I love it. There were dozens of guys sometimes, once nearly a hundred, a little counter on the screen told him how many, they would urge him on as he brought out his toys, ever larger dildos and plugs. It was never much money, he said, unless a guy wanted a private show, and then they could leave the site and go to Skype, and he might earn thirty or forty euro. But I don't really do it for the money, he said. Once he had auditioned to do porn, or not auditioned exactly, there had been a call on one of the websites he used and he had sent his photos to a company in Germany, but they didn't want me, he said, they didn't even send me a response. Can you believe it, I would have been amazing, they wouldn't even have to pay me, I would have been a star. Maybe it was to shock him out of his fantasy that when he moved forward to take me in his mouth I stopped him, catching his forehead in my palm. He objected, he made a little grunt, half protest and half question, bending his head back to look up at me. I grabbed his chin in my other hand and spread the hinge of his jaw wide. He let me do this, he looked up at me until, realizing what I intended, he shut his eyes and I spat hard into his mouth. He made another noise, this time of pleasure, and when I let him go he dove onto me, in a single movement taking my whole cock in his mouth, almost to the base, and again I nearly flinched, I bent myself just slightly around him and grabbed his head, not to force him down but just to hold him still, the sensation was too much. But the sensation didn't stop, I held his head in place but his tongue kept moving, he swallowed repeatedly so that it moved up and down, muscular and snakelike, and I found myself making a noise I hadn't intended to make, not just a noise but a word, I don't remember what it was, some expletive, shit or fuck, low and drawn out, a word that can mean anything and that meant here that it was wonderful, what he was doing, and it became more wonderful when I let his head go.

Everybody thinks they're good at sucking dick but they're not, usually, they don't cover their teeth or they make the same single motion again and again or they can't take it deep enough or there's something half-hearted about it, even guys who claim they love to suck, who pride themselves on it. But he was different, he was the best I had ever had, and I gave myself over to it, over to him, I forgot the role I was supposed to play and let him do whatever he wanted. I thought suddenly of a girl I knew when I was a kid, a very large girl who was my friend, unpopular except that she was famous for being easy, for letting anybody who wanted to have a go. I hadn't thought of her for years. The same boys who called her names at school would fuck her at night, fuck her or ask her to suck them, so that she had a public life where she was humiliated and a private life where she was desired. It was a kind of power, I suppose, or what felt like power, to both of us, we would talk on the phone and tell each other our adventures, hers in a boy's stinking car or bedroom, mine in the toilets or the park; you slut, we'd say to each other, laughing, you dirty whore. She was two years older than I was, sixteen, a junior at our school, and she liked to call herself my teacher, though by that time really I think I had had more sex than she had; in a single night at the park I could have three or four guys, it didn't take long for me to catch up. But it was the form our friendship took, that I was her student, that she would teach me how to be a whore. You have to be in love with them, she told me once, each one, you might hate them other times but you have to love them when you're giving head, you have to imagine that you can never tell them, that the only way you can say it is by how you suck them. You have to give everything, she said, that's the only way to give a blowjob. I hadn't thought of her for years but I thought of her now, because that was how he sucked, taking me as deep as he could and then kissing the tip, taking my balls in his mouth, rubbing his face against me until it shone with his own saliva. It was a kind of love, or what felt like love, reverence maybe, worship, and it filled me up with something like pride, though that's not the right word for it, something like arrogance or aggression, maybe that's the way to put it, I felt myself becoming what he wanted. I urged him on, I said That's right, suck that cock, the language of porn that's so ridiculous unless you're lit up with a longing that makes it the most beautiful language in the world, full of meaning, profound, do you like that cock, I asked, but it wasn't really a question, or it was a question he had already answered, show me how much you love it. And he did, he wasn't just using his mouth, he was using his hands, too, rubbing my balls and stroking the shaft slick with his saliva, he was learning what I liked.

He couldn't quite take it all, the position wasn't right, he twisted his head to come at it from different angles but the bend in his throat blocked it. Finally he stopped trying, he sat back on his knees and then stood, a breach of contract, which he acknowledged by saying Sorry, and then, can you lie down, he asked, it will be better that way. He took me by the arm and turned me toward the makeshift bed against the wall. I did as he asked, feeling how thin the little mattress was, less a mattress than a pad of some sort, like the mats laid out in a gym; later I would think about the uncomfortable nights he must spend there. I lay on my back, bunching his pillow beneath my head, and he climbed up next to me. He got on his side in the opposite direction, his head toward my feet. He half straddled me, placing a hand on either side of my waist but keeping both knees to one side, not quite the position Whitman says the soul assumes in relation to the body (I wouldn't be sucking him, I still hadn't touched his cock), and then, in a single quick, almost violent motion, he swallowed me. He had been right to move us, he could take it all now, and I groaned at the sensation of entering his throat, the tightness of the passage there. He forced himself down, pressing his chin into my pubic bone, his nose into my balls, and then put his hands on my hips and pulled me toward him, urging my pelvis up. I had been too passive, I realized, it wasn't really what he wanted, he wanted me to act. And so I took his head in my hands and started fucking his face, pulling him toward me and lifting my hips, taking all his art from him, all or nearly all. When you're being used like that you become an object, which is the pleasure of it, your only role is to be the best object you can be, to keep your lips wrapped around your teeth, to curl your tongue to make the right aperture, now tighter and now more ample; you have to become a hole, which was what he had said he wanted. I went easy at first, since most men say they want it but they don't really, they gag or choke and they've had enough; it's another fantasy of themselves, what they think they want they don't actually want. But he was different, he took it without complaint, and so I fucked him harder, I gripped him more tightly and bent his neck this way and that, trying different angles. Finally he did gag, for the first time, not just in his throat but deep in his abdomen, and I let him go. But he didn't want to be let go, he grabbed my knees with both of his hands and locked them around his head, not letting me pull away. Something came over me again, that intensity or aggression I had felt earlier, a kind of cruelty, and I said Take it then, almost spitting the words, gripping the back of his head and fucking it hard, in short savage thrusts as he gagged, take it, and then I held it in place, pulling him against me as his body jerked, and I took pleasure in his suffering, in his willingness to suffer. It was the pleasure of being a man, I think, I'm not sure I had ever felt it before. I luxuriated in it, I didn't want to let him go, I held him even after he motioned for me to stop, I let go only when he started slapping at my thighs. He took great gulps of air, hanging his head above my cock, threads of saliva still connecting us, viscous and heavy, until he used one hand to wipe his face. So good, he said then, his voice thick, so fucking good, and he smiled at me before he started sucking me again.

I dropped my head back on the pillow, letting him work. He spread his legs a little, revealing his asshole, which was hairless and clean, beautiful, and which moved gently, maybe he wasn't aware of it, it tightened and relaxed like the mouth of some primitive creature, all appetite. I placed my thumb over it and he moaned again and tightened it more, so that it kissed me, almost, or made as if to swallow me, it invited me in. Even without lube it was easy to enter him, he relaxed and took my thumb to the first knuckle without any strain at all, and then he tightened again around me. He pushed back, tilting his pelvis slightly. But I couldn't go deeper, or not easily, I could only apply pressure in and out, encouraging his own movement, his rocking back and forth. But it wasn't enough, for him or for me. He stopped sucking me when I pulled my thumb free, raising his head and looking back, and then opening his mouth for my thumb, which he sucked at eagerly, as he did the first two fingers of the same hand when I presented them, taking both at the same time, moving his head to take them deeper, as far as they would reach. I lifted my head to spit on his hole, rubbing it in a way meant to give pleasure, and then gave him my whole thumb, to the second joint, and then, since he had taken it so easily, immediately starting his back and forth motion, I inserted my first two fingers at once, together, not quite gently, pressing them in a single motion to the base.

This gave him pause, he arched his back, taking a moment before he began to fuck himself again, fucking himself at both ends, pressing back on my fingers and then diving down on my cock. I pressed forward as he moved back, withdrew to the second knuckle or even the first when he moved forward, each of us meeting the other in our movement until it became a single movement, a movement meant for his pleasure though there was something savage in it, too, the way he moaned when on every third or fourth thrust I twisted my wrist, stretching him; he made a sound that wasn't as sharp as a cry but that wasn't entirely of pleasure, I liked making him make that sound. I could feel him moving against me, not just forward and back but pressing around my fingers as well, making himself tighter and then giving way. He was showing me what he could do, I thought, how good he was at getting fucked. He had meant every word of it, what he had said about himself online, I wasn't sure I had ever met anyone who embodied so fully his fantasy of himself. I thought of all the men who had fucked him, adding a third finger to the two already inside, feeling again that strange tenderness for him, even as I twisted my hand to give him the pain he wanted, as I thrust my hips up to gag him. Why should I care who fucks me, he would say to me later, why should I say no to anybody, I don't want to say no. Why shouldn't I give it away, his body, he meant, what could I do with it that would be better? I like for guys to fuck me, who cares if they're ugly or old, I hate all that, people who think they're so special nobody deserves to fuck them. Why should you have to deserve it, he would say, his head on my chest, who doesn't deserve a little fucking? I think we should all give it away, wouldn't it be wonderful, everyone fucking all the time, everywhere, I would love it, and I laughed, I said I would too, it would be my version of heaven. And when I asked him if he worried about disease he said Fuck worrying, I hate it, I don't want to worry. I don't want to live forever, I'd rather live ten years the way I want than live forever and be miserable, I want to be happy. I don't care about being safe, he said, I don't care if I get sick, why should I be special, and I wondered what feeling he was speaking from, whether it was joy or defiance or despair, I wanted to know where one ended and the others began. I wanted to argue with him, but I didn't argue, what would have been the use, and anyway to argue with him would have been to lay claim to him somehow, to violate his ethics of claimlessness. Because it was an ethics, I thought as I lay with him, it was more coherent than my own life, with its alternating precaution and risk; I tried to imagine his life of wholeheartedness but I knew it would never be mine.

It was about joy, the story he would tell me, but it wasn't joy I saw as he moved back and forth between my cock and my hand, or not only joy. I had the sense that he was looking for something and not finding it, making his movements sharper and faster; he was asking a question I didn't know how to answer, that I tried to answer by jabbing my hand and twisting it with each movement he made. But he was frustrated, I thought, and finally he stopped his motion, he forced himself down on my cock, taking me as deep as he could, shaking his head a little as if to work me in deeper, like a dog worrying a toy. I used my free hand to grab his head and fucked him as hard as I could, savagely, in a way meant to hurt him. I tilted slightly on my side and wrapped my legs around his head, trapping him and moving my hips very fast, as hard and as fast as I could, an uncontrolled motion, a kind of spasm to echo his own spasm as he choked on me, though even as he choked he locked his arms around my ass, to keep me from pulling away. I made a sound then too, loud and guttural, almost a shout, and it was only when I heard it that I realized it was anger I felt, hot and eager, I didn't know where it came from but I would make him feel it too, I thought. I held him in place even as I felt him try to pull his head back, even after he started slapping my thighs again I held him down. I wanted to frighten him, I think, I wanted it not to be a game. You want it, I said as he struggled, you want it, take it then, I said, take it, you fucking whore, and it was the shock of the words that made me let him go, the words and what I felt as I said them.

I pulled my fingers from him (slowly now, gently), and he grabbed my hand and brought it to his mouth, cleaning it though it wasn't dirty, he was immaculate, he had cleaned himself out before I arrived. As he lay on his side gasping he said again So fucking good, not smiling now, and I thought I had satisfied him. But when he stood I saw he wasn't satisfied, his cock was still hard as he stepped across the room and bent over to pick up the coil of my belt. I sat up as he held it out, and when I didn't take it he said I want you to beat me, his voice neutral, matter-of-fact, I want you to whip me with it. I swung my legs off the bed but didn't get up, I hesitated before finally taking the belt from him and standing. This hadn't been part of the scene we had planned, he hadn't said he wanted it, I wasn't sure it was a scene I liked. He knelt on the bed again, on his hands and knees, presenting his ass. I stepped to the foot of the bed, letting the belt unroll from my hand, then taking the tip again to fold it, I would strike him with half its length. I had never whipped anyone before but that was how my father had done it, taking the strap to us, as he said, that was how he punished us. I took the folded belt in both hands and brought my hands together, making the halves bend out like wings, and then snapped it quickly twice, the noise loud in the small room, making me flinch. That too was what my father had always done, frightening us to double our punishment, I guess, to make us fear the belt before we felt it. At the sound of it he shifted his position, he lowered his torso, dropping to his elbows and resting his head on his clasped hands. I delayed a little more, I rubbed his ass with my free hand, gripping the flesh. Then I struck him, not gently but I knew he could feel my reluctance, and after a second and a third time he said Harder, his voice muffled against his hands, and then again, harder, and I obeyed, striking him each time with greater force, warming into it. But still he said Harder after each stroke, almost like a taunt, and I didn't know whether it was in response to his voice or to my movement that I became cruel again, became all acquiescence, I would punish him if it was punishment he wanted. I would tan his hide, I thought, which was another thing my father said when he beat us, I'll tan your hide; he said it with the voice he used only when he was very angry, the voice of his childhood, his country voice. Maybe it was the same anger I felt, that hot thing that filled me up as I struck him again and again, I would shut him up, I thought, though I didn't shut him up, he still spoke as I beat him, saying Yes after each stroke, yes, yes, and this made me angry, too, I can't say why, it stoked the hot feeling that made me strike him harder. Shut up, I thought, though I didn't speak the words, shut the fuck up, and it made me glad when he stopped saying yes, when he made other noises instead, inarticulate, animal, when he stopped giving me permission; maybe that was it, I didn't want his permission, we had gotten past permission, I thought. I was hard again, beating him had made me hard; I didn't know I could enjoy someone's suffering that way but I did enjoy it, I wanted him to suffer more. When my arm was tired I raised it above my head, my right arm, and brought it down harder, not on his ass but on his back, which I struck three times very fast and with all my strength. He cried out sharply, a cry of real pain, pinched and high-pitched, but he didn't break his position, he stayed crouched with his hands clasped beneath his head. Nor did he move when I dropped the belt and climbed onto the bed behind him. I had thought I wouldn't fuck him but I wanted to fuck him now, I had to do it, it was a kind of compulsion, a necessary conclusion to what he had made me feel, I needed to be inside him. His ass was red from the beating, it was hot to the touch when I smacked him, which elicited another cry, more of surprise than of pain, I thought. I spit into the same hand and slicked my cock with it, just a little; I knew I was close, if I stroked myself too hard I would come too soon, and also I didn't want to be too slick, I wanted him to feel it. I had opened him up already, he would still be wet from my hand, but I didn't want it to be too easy for him, I wanted it to hurt.

I lined myself up and then hesitated, remembering my earlier worries about disease, the men who had fucked him and me, it was a stupid risk; but then he leaned back until he touched my cock, his hole tightening like a mouth again, and I didn't care about disease, about disease or anything else, if there was a risk we would share that too, and in a single motion I made him take it all. I held still for a moment, waiting for the pleasure to dull. When I pulled back he tightened against me, his body straining to hold me in, and then I took his narrow pelvis in both hands and fucked him hard. Yes, he said again, yes, but it didn't annoy me now, it had become sweet to me, I liked it when he said Fuck me, when he said fuck me harder, that inane dialogue; I'll fuck you, I said, I'll fuck you hard, take it, I said, pulling on him as I thrust forward, slamming him against me. He had lifted himself onto his hands again, and he arched his back, pushing into me. Like that, he said, like that, make me your whore, and I laughed a little, I said Is that what you want, you want to be my whore? I slapped him then, hard on his ass, and he groaned, Please, he said, his voice electric with need, please, fuck me like your whore, I want to be your faggot whore, and at the sound of it I felt something move in me, like a shifting of gears. That's right, I said, you're my faggot whore, and then I shoved him down, hard, and fell on top of him, pinning him beneath my weight. I hooked my arm beneath his neck and pulled his face close to mine, choking him, You faggot, I said, fucking him more slowly but more savagely, digging into him, you worthless faggot. My voice was low now, I was speaking into his ear, You know what you are, I said, you're a whore, this is all you're good for, I said, this is all you deserve. Maybe they had always been there, these words, maybe once you have heard such language it infects you, that was what it felt like, like something bursting free in me, corrosive and hot, without end, I had been waiting my entire life to say those words. I lifted my head and spat on his face, twice in quick succession, saying Faggot each time, you dirty faggot, and he cried out again, his eyes clenched shut. I smeared the saliva on his face and left my hand on his head, leaning on him, forcing his face into the thin mattress, against the hard wood beneath it. Please, he said again, his voice muffled, please, I'm nothing. He repeated this, I'm nothing, I'm nothing, and I echoed him, I said That's right, I was fucking him with my whole body, lifting up and falling back on him, you're a faggot, I said, you're nothing, you're a faggot, you're nothing. I hammered into him as I felt it rise in me, that cruelty and rage, that acid grief, and when I came I felt him come beneath me, his body shaking, I heard him give a cry of joy.

I hung over him, letting him grow still, then pulled out and fell onto my back beside him. *Mnogo hubavo beshe*, he said, that was good, speaking Bulgarian for the first time, his face turned away. When I didn't answer he turned toward me, then lifted himself onto his side. Hey, he said, his voice solicitous, hey. I put my hand over my face, which was wet with tears. I was embarrassed, I didn't want him to see me, when he asked what was wrong I couldn't answer. Stop it, he said, pulling my hand away, stop it, which made me cry harder somehow, and he kissed me, my forehead and cheeks, my lips, when I tried to pull away he grabbed my head with both his hands, holding me in place. *Sladurche*, he said, sweet boy, stop it now, don't be like that, and then he licked my face, quickly, playfully, like a cat, everywhere he had kissed he licked, catching my hands in his when I tried to shield myself or push him away, until I was laughing and weeping both, I stopped struggling and let him lick my face. He laughed too, rolling on top of me, still licking me, and I realized that I had been wrong before; it did have an end, what I had felt, its end was here, he had brought me here. Finally he laid his head on my chest. Don't be like that, he said again as I put my arms around him. Do you see? You don't have to be like that, he said. You can be like this.

AN EVENING OUT

Z. had emptied half the carton of juice, and now I was holding it as he poured the vodka into the plastic funnel at the top. We had laughed at the way he threw his head back and drank, sucking the juice down even as he grimaced at the taste, which was sickly sweet. He refused to dump it in the gutter: My grandfather was Russian, he said, we never waste anything. And that too had made us laugh, though he was serious now as he poured, tilting the plastic flask to let the barest ribbon of liquid thread perfectly into the carton. He didn't want to waste that, either, and I was so absorbed in holding the carton still—and absorbed in Z., too, who stood close to me, our shoulders almost touching—that I had nearly forgotten about N. when I heard the click of his phone as it took a picture of us. What are you doing, I said, and I'm sure there was a note in my voice of real concern at the thought of the image shared with others, but we had already drunk enough that the concern was distant, and N. laughed it off. I'm sorry, he said, it's just too epic, we've been waiting for this for so long. He laughed again when I warned him not to post it on Facebook. I'll hunt you down, I said, one of the phrases I had used often in my seven years as a teacher. He held up his hands, smiling broadly. Don't worry, he said, I won't, I just want to remember this forever.

Z. took the carton from me and screwed the lid back on, shaking it vigorously and for far too long, making us laugh again. It was the second flask of vodka, the second carton of juice, the second time Z. had taken in hand the mixing of our drinks. He would have poured for us if we had had anything to use as cups; instead we drank straight from the carton, which he handed to me first and then to N. before drinking from it himself. We were on a narrow street in the city center, standing beneath a streetlamp in front of the little twenty-four-hour shop where we had bought our supplies. It was already late, but we had an hour or so before the concert at the club that was our real destination. Sofia is famous for these clubs, where the city's wealthy dance and drink; they're called *chalgoteki*, after the pop-folk music they play. I had never been to one before. But now, since I was leaving Sofia, Z. had insisted that at least once I should have what he called a real Bulgarian night out, and the lure of him had overcome all my aversion to drunkenness and noise. I was eager for it, even, I planned to enjoy myself, to dance and drink, to relax in the company of these boys I genuinely liked, to be their friend for an evening and not their teacher.

The evening had started a few hours before, at a restaurant where I had promised to meet a group of students to say goodbye. They were already there when I arrived, ten or twelve of them seated at tables they had pushed together.

When they saw me several of them stood up, their chairs scraping on the uneven patio, and they called out my name, or not my name really but my family name, I mean my father's name; soon I wouldn't be that name anymore, I thought, feeling suddenly the relief of it. Of course it was what they called me, though they weren't students anymore, or not my students; they had graduated a year earlier and were back in Sofia after their first year abroad, in America or England or Amsterdam, they had scattered as all my students here scatter, none of them had stayed behind. There was already wine on the table, three bottles opened to breathe, a cheap Bulgarian white for the late June evening, even as I took my seat I could taste the twinge of it. But it was a pleasure to hold it up to the light, and more than a pleasure to hear them say my name again, my father's name, and then Z. said To new beginnings, and we drank. It was terrible wine but it didn't matter, I was as happy in that moment as I had ever been. There were more toasts over dinner, as the waiters carried out dishes that my students had missed while they were away, salads and grilled meats and ceramic pots of vegetables and cheese. They toasted one another, their year away, their stories of London and New York.

I had a fucking miserable year, N. said when his turn came, I mean I knew it would be awful but it was fucking miserable. I told you, Z. said, I knew you weren't cut out to be a lawyer, and the girl next to him said That's true, and everyone at the table loudly agreed, making N. raise his hands in surrender. Hey, he said, I wasn't the one who wanted it, but even *Gospodinut*—and here he waved one of his hands toward me—couldn't convince my mother it was a terrible idea. It was true that I had tried, at the beginning of N.'s senior year, when his mother came in for her quarterly conference. She never missed these meetings, even though it meant a two-hour drive from her home in Plovdiv, losing half a day of work. She was a serious woman, invariably dressed in a pants suit, dark navy or gray, her black hair cut in a severe line just above her shoulders. She was gracious, too, and she had thanked me once for my influence, as she put it; You are the only teacher he works hard for, she said, this is the only class he likes. He isn't a stupid boy, she said, as she always did when we discussed his poor grades, his late or missing assignments, but oh, he is so lazy. But this time I demurred, It isn't exactly that he's lazy, I said. I saw her face tighten slightly with the wariness I often saw in parents when I began to speak about their children, a knitting of the brow that might have meant a special kind of attention but was usually the opposite, was usually their attention shutting down. When N. is interested he will work, I said, if it's something he likes — and here she turned her head to the side, she made a thick sound with her tongue in the back of her throat. Please, N.'s mother said, turning back to me, her tone at once dismissive and imploring, please, if he likes it? What will he do when he has a job, he can't only work when he wants to. I nodded and started to speak but she went on, Please, she said, I know what you will say, N. has told me many times, you tell them they should do what they love, it's beautiful what you tell them. I see why they like you so much, she said, with a tight, conciliatory smile.

I do tell them that, I said, I believe it. I took a breath. He has a talent, I said, I think he's lucky to have found it, and yes, I think he should follow what he loves and build his life around it. I paused. I had been wringing my hands beneath the table, knitting and unknitting my fingers, and now I laid them flat on top of it. I worry about N. in law school, I said, I worry that he will keep doing badly. I think, and here I tried to make my voice lighter somehow, I think he should do what he feels called to do, I think he should study what he wants. She sat very still as I spoke, her tight smile unchanging. Yes, she said again, it's very beautiful what you say, very inspiring. And what does he do then, she said, after he studies what he wants, what does he do when he has to get a job? Things are different here, *Gospodine*, maybe in America what you say is true; you try something there and if you fail it is no problem, you try something else, Americans love starting over, you say it's never too late. But for us it is always too late, she said. When N. gets his diploma he has to find a job, right away, a good job in England, if he doesn't he has to come back here, and if he comes back here it will be very hard for him to leave again, do you understand, if he comes back here he will be trapped. I know you care about him, she said, settling back in her chair, I know your heart, and she hesitated, groping for the phrase, your heart is in the right place, but what you say isn't true for us, please, you must help him see that. N. groaned when I repeated this to him the next morning at school. You see, he said, she won't listen, it's impossible to talk to her. It's because she loves you, I said, it's a way of loving you, and he sighed and looked away.

Well, N. said at the restaurant table, lowering his hands before Z. interrupted him—Listen up, *Gospodine*, he said, you're going to like this. N. smiled at me. No more law school, he said, I'm transferring, in the fall I'll be doing literature. There was a cheer around the table, as several students said *Chestito*, congratulations, and all of us raised our glasses. But what about your mother, I asked after we drank, how did you convince her? N.'s smile widened. It was easy, he said, I just failed all my classes, and everyone laughed. I don't approve of your methods, I said, though I was laughing too, and Z. raised his glass and said To whatever works, and we toasted again.

We toasted on the street, too, after a fashion, lifting the carton to one another before we drank. This had been our plan, to leave the others after dinner and drink together, just the three of us, a prelude to more drinking at the club. We passed the carton as we walked the narrow streets, but the second or third time it made the circuit I handed it directly to Z. Hey, he said, trying to give it back to me, you can't skip your turn. But I didn't take it. I need to slow down, I said, I can't drink as much as you. I was already feeling it, the wine from earlier and the vodka we were drinking too quickly now, I could feel the edges of myself softening, a kind of tingling, like a limb waking up. It was dangerous to drink so much; I didn't have a sense of who I would be if I got really drunk, I had never let myself go like that, as men around me did in my childhood, it was another way I had always been unlike them. *Gospodine*, Z. said, his voice heavy with disappointment, come on now, and he shook the carton, still holding it out to me, don't let us down. All right, I said, relenting. And then, in a broad, cartoonish Slavic accent, another classroom trick, I said Tonight I make exception, and drank deeply. Bravo, Z. said, that's the way, and N. said again

This is so epic, and then, this is the best night of my life, which made all three of us laugh.

I hadn't been paying attention to where Z. was leading us, and I was surprised when we arrived at the Doctor's Garden, a little tree-filled park just west of the university. I had been there often, I loved it during the day, and at night it filled like all the parks with young people drinking. Let's stop for a minute, Z. said, pulling out his phone and making the little screen light up, we still had some time to kill before we needed to be at the club. Z. turned off the path almost as soon as we entered the park, taking us into a section of trees and grass that was filled with dozens of fragments of marble, broken pillars and bits of cornices. This part of the garden was dark, and the stones glowed faintly, reflecting the light from the paths and playgrounds. I had looked at these fragments before, in the daytime, reading the plaques laid in the ground with information about their provenance, the various archaeological digs where they were found, translations of their inscriptions. Z. chose a pillar the right height and sat the carton on top of it, making me suck my breath between my teeth. What, he asked, and I said something about its antiquity, how it was thousands of years old and he was using it as his table. N. laughed. All this time in Bulgaria, he said, and you're still such an American. We have stuff like this everywhere, he said, if we couldn't touch it we couldn't live. And besides, Z. said, don't you think it's better out here than in a museum, I think it likes it, and he ran his hand down the length of the stone, a strangely sensual gesture, I think it likes us to touch it. Go ahead, he said, you touch it too, and when I hesitated, he took my arm just above the wrist and pulled it to the stone. I laughed, surrendering, and stroked it as he had done, the stone warmer than the air, it must have soaked in the late sun, and pocked, not smooth at all, or smooth only where letters had been chiseled into it, the slanted edges of the cut still perfectly polished. I drew my hands away and wiped them on my jeans. The park was busy, not just with college students but with couples sitting on the benches that lined the paths, and with children playing on the swing sets and slides. Are you ready then, Z. said, taking the carton and unscrewing the cap, though I think we had all been relieved to leave it untouched for a while, everything packed for your move, and I said it was, more or less, there were still a few days before I would leave. Will you miss it, N. asked, meaning the country, I thought, or maybe teaching, and I said I would, of course, how could he wonder.

There was a loud sound then from a distance, an air horn, followed by a single low drum beaten very fast, the sound of a few people making as much noise as they could. Are they still at it, I asked, and Z. nodded, A few of them, they'll be out all night. There had been huge protests weeks before, but the heart went out of them as time passed and nothing changed, the government refused to resign and the protest-ers melted away until only a few dozen remained, circling the city each night as they shouted slogans. *Neshtastnitsi*, Z. said, assholes. Why, I asked him, what do you mean, and he shrugged. What do they think will happen, he said, nothing will change here, I don't even think they care who's in the government, it's just a game. And these guys, he went on, his voice bitter now, their drums, sleeping in tents, they're just playing a game too, it doesn't matter, they can't find jobs so this is how they spend their time. N. groaned. Fuck, he said, that's going to be me in a few years, and Z. laughed. It will not, I said, reaching across to put my hand on his shoulder, leaning forward too far, I had to put my other hand on the pillar again to keep my balance. You'll be fine, I said, looking at him, do your work and don't be scared, that's all, it's all you can do. He shrugged as I removed my hand, placing it beside the other on the stone. I don't know, he said, my mom is probably right, I don't have any idea what I'll do after college, I'll probably have to come back here and be a bum. Z. laughed again, picking up the carton in a kind of toast. Job security, he said, there will always be bums, and N. groaned again.

Let's go, Z. said, checking the time, and he set off quickly through the park, so that N. and I struggled to keep up. *E, kopele*, N. said, bastard, slow down, why are you rushing, and Z. turned and smiled, still walking, moving backward along the street. We don't want to be late, we'll miss the show, he said. He made a motion with his hips, a little Turkish shimmy, before he turned back around. The club was a short walk away, on Tsar Osvoboditel, part of a complex that housed one of the city's most luxurious hotels. We showed our *lichni karti* to the two men stationed at the door, their torsos obscene with muscle, and then descended a long carpeted staircase that was lit dimly by red lights set high along the walls. There were mirrors mounted every few feet, and I found myself stealing glances as we passed, seeing how incongruous a group we made, wondering what people would make of my presence with these men so much younger than I, still boys really. The music got louder as we approached the glass doors separating the corridor from the club proper, and it overwhelmed me as Z. pulled them open and we stepped through into a cavernous, dark room strafed by lights that spun somewhere above us. The air was heavy with cigarette smoke, abrasive as sand, despite the new law that had passed months before; I could see it hanging beneath the only steady illumination, above the bar in the center of the room, where four men in identical black suits were mixing drinks. We made our way single file through the crowded space, toward the corner farthest from the entrance, where there were a few unclaimed tables, small and chest-high, each with an ashtray and an unopened bottle of gin. Nearer the bar people stood with bottles and glasses, moving their shoulders and hips, dancing in place. There wasn't a dance floor, though what else could be the point of the place; the music was so loud it was almost impossible to talk, after only a minute of it my ears ached.

A young woman walked over to us, holding a tray above her head as she angled her way through the crowd. She wore a white blouse several sizes too small, exposing her navel and buttoned just barely above her breasts, which she allowed to touch Z., casually erotic, as she leaned over and brought her face to his. She shouted something into his ear as she placed three glasses and a small bucket of ice on the table. He reciprocated her gesture, putting an arm around her shoulder, and N. and I looked at each other and laughed. Z. was always theatrical with women, a cartoon Lothario at sixteen who had grown into real seduction; it was like he breathed sex as he exchanged comments with the server, they could almost have been kissing as they moved mouth to ear. But then Z. drew back, letting his arm fall from her shoulder, and looked at her in disbelief. He jerked his head in a single vertical motion, a decided no. He started to turn toward N. but the waitress pressed her hand to his chest and gestured for him to come back. She spoke longer this time, her hand on his chest, balancing the empty tray on the table. Now Z. did turn to N., shouting into his ear, and N. shouted to me in turn that to stay at the table we had to buy the gin. Okay, I shouted back, how much, and when he told me 160 leva, 80 euro, I burst out laughing, making Z. and N. laugh, too. But the woman didn't laugh, she shrugged, all her seductiveness gone. It's crazy, Z. shouted, but the alternative was to stand in the packed space between the bar and the booths, where you could hardly breathe, what would be the point of that, and so I pulled out my billfold. One night, I said, my throat already raw with shouting and with smoke, and they smiled and pulled out their wallets. No no, I said, wagging my forefinger, I didn't want them to spend their money. I had gone to the *bankomat* earlier that day, my wallet was full of bills, and I drew out several to hand to the woman, who smiled again, opening the gin and a can of tonic and pouring us our first drinks before she spun away.

There were maybe seven or eight tables in our corner of the room, almost all of them taken by groups of young people, some of them high school students, I thought, two or three couples gathered at each. N. waved to catch our attention, then pointed back to the entrance, nodding to Z. before he left. Z. mouthed something at me but I didn't understand, the music was too loud, and after he repeated it to no avail he dropped his hands to his crotch and mimed a man pissing, his hand curled as if around an impossibly large cock. I laughed, both because it was funny and because it hid the other thing I felt. I mocked him, first holding my hand up, curled like his, making a doubtful face, and then I dropped both hands to my own crotch, as if holding a cock twice as large, three times, and Z. laughed too, a genuine laugh, I thought, though it wasn't very funny, and both of us seemed a little embarrassed once the laughter had passed. Then Z. said something else and again I didn't understand, so he took his phone out of his pocket and typed, holding up the screen for me to read. This is a great night, he had written, and I looked up and said Yes, and we raised our glasses, clinking them before we drank.

The music changed as we set our glasses down, there was a sudden assault of *gaidi*, the mountain bagpipes ubiquitous in Balkan folk music, and then a syncopated rush of drums that made both of us grin. It was a song we knew well, one of the big hits of Z.'s senior year, and we lifted our glasses again, toasting each other and the song and the memory of it we had. With the glass still at his lips Z. began to dance, he extended his other arm away from his body and twisted slightly from side to side, and though it was half ironic it made me feel a kind of pang, since it was for me, his dance, I was his only audience, it could only be for me. After a few seconds, he put his glass down, dropping his other arm too, abandoning his performance. But I raised my own arms, awkward and un-American, I shuffled a step toward him and he was in it again. It was like I had given him permission to dance, to be foolish in front of me, since I was so much more foolish, without his beauty or his youth, I was an old man in this place. But he smiled at me and I smiled back and we were dancing with each other, after a fashion, we made a little orbit together, a center of gravity. At one point I reached over and put my hand on his shoulder, a friendly gesture, casual, avuncular maybe, and then I let my hand slide down his arm and, as I felt him flex his bicep, that reflexive preening, I curled my fingers around the muscle there and squeezed, feeling how solid it was. I knew the gesture wasn't casual anymore, that it showed too much, I was touching him as I had never allowed myself to touch a student before. But he wasn't my student, I told myself, for one night we could face each other without all that, I could touch his arm and have all of that fall away. Or maybe that's not what I thought, maybe I'm adding it now, maybe then all I felt was a seam or line drawn taut from my throat to my groin, a circuit that came alive in contact with him. He smiled and bent his arm at the elbow, pumping the muscle, and I let my other hand join the first, linking my fingers around his arm to take in the full span of it. I had stopped dancing, I realized, and I dropped my hands as I felt the embarrassment of admiring him for too long. But he didn't seem embarrassed, he didn't stop smiling, though he wasn't dancing anymore, either; he stopped to slide his hand into the front pocket of his jeans, which were tight, my eyes followed as he worked his fingers in and slid out his phone. His face was studious in the light cast by the screen, and then he held it up and I saw that he had typed in all caps IRON MAN. He expected me to laugh but I didn't laugh, I looked at him, past the glare of the phone which must have been lighting my face now, letting him read whatever he could see there, I looked and shook my head from right to left in affirmation; *Da*, I said, though he couldn't hear me or the tone in which I said it, which was a serious tone, grave, *Da*. He slid the phone back in his pocket, smiling more broadly, and took a step toward me. He squared himself off, facing me and planting both his feet, like a challenge, and then he balled one of his hands into a fist and struck his own stomach twice, hard, showing off the muscles there, too, before he opened his hand to make a welcoming gesture, jerking his head up in invitation. He wanted me to try, and when I didn't immediately strike him he reached out and grabbed my wrist, pulling it toward his stomach. I made a fist and let him strike himself with it, he *was* like iron, I thought, or like something more precious, like marble, and when he gestured for me to hit him again, harder, I did hit him, not very hard but hard enough to satisfy him. I left my hand there, my knuckles flush with his abdomen, and then I opened my hand and laid my palm flat against his stomach, the cotton of his shirt just slightly damp with sweat, and let my fingers trace the muscles there, risen in their rows as he clenched them, I curved the ends of my fingers around them and pressed against them as long as I dared. Then I released my grip and smiled and brushed his stomach quickly up and down with the back of my hand, as if to erase the trace of how I had touched him. I took my glass from the table and with a grimace drank what was left.

The same song was still playing, only a couple of minutes had passed. As soon as I set my glass down Z. was filling it, gallant again, and then N. was back from the bathroom, lifting his own glass expectantly, so Z. filled it, too, and then his own, and once more we were toasting one another. I glanced around, aware that everything I had felt would have been obvious to anyone watching us, but no one was watching us; in the dim light I could see the other tables and beyond them the crowded floor unchanged. I put my arm around N.'s shoulders, friendly, trying to normalize touch, and he and I danced a little. Another song had come on, one I didn't know but that didn't matter, you can always dance to *chalga*, that's the whole point of it, its single virtue. I had turned away from Z. to dance with N., who wasn't a good dancer at all, he didn't even try to dance well: he made all his movements ironic, self-deprecating, an extension of the persona he had taken on in class, which was endearing but also a product of uncertainty or doubt, a kind of abnegation. I wanted him to grow out of it but now I played along, laughing, dancing in the same way, our motions silly and shuffling, a game that was in a way the opposite of eros and so a relief to me.

I had only lost track of him for a minute or two, but when I looked over again Z. had disappeared. He must have gone to the bathroom, I thought, and immediately I stopped dancing. I shouted to N. that I was going to piss, at which he nodded, and I left him without a thought for how odd it was, to leave him there alone, how transparent it must have been, I would think of it only later. I moved as quickly as I could, twisting through the crowd, finding openings between the groups of drinkers; I wasn't so drunk, I thought. I had almost reached an open space near the entrance when I stumbled into a man's back. He turned quickly, muscular and affronted, but smiled when I held up both hands in apology, *Izvinyavaite*, pardon me, *suzhalyavam*, I'm sorry, and he put a large hand on my shoulder and squeezed, friendly and forgiving, welcoming me into the camaraderie of happy drinking. And then in the dimness ahead there was a sudden rectangle of porcelain light as a door opened and I was in a large bright room, tiled and clean. There were three urinals along one wall, and a man was stepping away from one of them, zipping himself up. Z. was still there, I saw with relief, I wasn't too late, and I stepped up beside him, breaking that distributive propriety of men's bathrooms, a guard against unchecked glances, against desire. He looked over and saw it was me and smiled, a little blurrily, I thought, he was drunker than I was, or drunker than I felt, and then he faced forward again. I didn't face forward, though I could have, I could still have seen what I wanted to see. I let my eyes track down his front, following the line of buttons down his shirt, which was ridiculous in the fluorescent light, a kind of garish violet. Even in my excitement I admired the neatness of it, the buttons perfectly aligned, and I thought for the first time in many years of my father dressing me as a boy, teaching me about this line, the gig line, he called it, buttons and buckle forming an order that was more than vanity, that signaled some deeper righteousness. The memory came in a flash before I let myself look at his cock, pale in his hand and pissing a pale line against the porcelain, nothing extraordinary, not small or particularly large, a handsome cock, and I felt my own stiffen a little when I saw that with his index finger he was rubbing just slightly the underside of the head, where he held the foreskin back, an unconscious gesture, probably, though it must have sent a small current of pleasure alongside the pleasure of pissing. I knew I was acting badly, that I was looking too brazenly and for too long, that I shouldn't have looked at all. I would be ashamed later but I wasn't ashamed now, I kept watching as the stream weakened and became intermittent, let him know, I said to myself, he already knows, let him see it. He let go of the head to pull the foreskin all the way back and shake himself before he pinched the base and drew his fingers up the shaft, stretching himself out to his full length and flicking off the drop of urine that hung at the tip. He did this two or three times and then stopped, leaving his cock dangling for a moment, in which I felt my excitement mount and become unbearable, he must be letting me look, I thought, it might be a kind of invitation, before he tucked himself away and drew up his fly.

Only then did I look up at his face. Our eyes met: he had been watching me or maybe he had only looked over at that instant, I don't know. He held my gaze without speaking, and I knew that if he gave any sign I would do whatever he wanted, or rather whatever he would let me do, I would go into one of the stalls with him or leave the club, walk out without a word to N., I didn't care, whatever he wanted I would do. He closed his eyes and swayed slightly before opening them again. Then he leaned toward me, crossing into my space, and said I'm really drunk, nearly shouting it, the music was loud in the bathroom, too. He leaned away again. Let's listen to the concert and then go home, he said and turned, walking to the sink to run water over his hands before going back into the club. I didn't follow right away, I stayed at the urinal, waiting for my excitement to settle, until the door opened and another man walked in, a fat man in an expensive suit, who stationed himself at a urinal beside me and with a sigh began to piss.

N. and Z. were standing at the table, not dancing anymore,

with full glasses in front of them, and as I joined them Z. refilled my glass, too. He was smiling, there wasn't any sign of what had happened as we knocked glasses, holding each other's eyes to say *Nazdrave*, I looked for some special message from him but there was none. While we were drinking, the music abruptly tapered and cut off, leaving a kind of roaring in its wake. And then over the speakers a man's voice, loud and deep, theatrical, said *Dami i gospoda*, ladies and gentlemen, and in a burst of quick syllables I couldn't quite follow announced Andrea, the singer we had come to see. With a single beat on a drum the lights snapped out, and with another drumbeat a stage I hadn't noticed was suddenly bathed in white light. It was against the opposite wall, on the other side of the bar, though we could see just fine, it wasn't as large a space as I had thought. A roar went up when the music started, the intro of Andrea's most popular song, "Haide opa," and another when a door in the wall opened and she stepped out onto the stage, followed by four other women. They wore skimpy two-piece outfits that exposed their midriffs, the four dancers almost identical, Andrea set off by what looked like a fur vest, plush and white, hanging open around her breasts, and by her hair, which wasn't gathered back like the others' but teased into a blond mane. It was a small stage, they could hardly move, they lifted their arms and spun, sometimes bending their knees deeply, everything exaggeratedly sexual. We had moved from our spots around the table and were standing in front of it, Z. in the middle, dancing so that we knocked into each other, our shoulders and hips, and then Z. put his arms around our shoulders and drew us tight, hugging us. When I looked over he was smiling, watching Andrea, smiling more when he turned his head and looked at me, and I smiled back, happy, pressing against him, reaching around him to squeeze N.'s shoulder, and he smiled at me too.

The women onstage struck a pose as the song ended, and then the music shifted, became even more frenetic, a song I didn't know, though there was another shout of recognition from the crowd. N. and Z. had always claimed they didn't like *chalga* but they shouted too, a little hurrah, and started to dance with more enthusiasm, lifting their arms in the air. I stepped away to give Z. more room, but he hooked one of his arms around my shoulder and pulled me close again, making me dance alongside him, his flank hot against mine, his arm hot against my back, and I felt myself swept by a wave of happiness, my face stretched stupidly in a grin. I must look foolish, I thought, but there was so much pleasure in being a fool, why had I spent so much of my life guarding against it? I looked at Z. and N. and saw my feeling mirrored back at me, their faces shone in the dark, or that's how I remember it, as though they were caught in the flare of a camera's flash. But no one was taking pictures, it's only my imagination that casts such light on them. On the stage, Andrea was pacing back and forth, like a cat in a cage. And then Z. stumbled beside me, he lost his footing and fell, or almost fell, gripping my shoulder so I was pulled forward with him, and I reached around with my other arm to catch him around the waist. Whoa, I said, struggling to hold him up as just for a second he was a dead weight in my arms. Then he found his footing, and as he unfolded himself to stand up again I saw that my hand had fallen to his crotch. I don't think I willed it, not exactly, I think it was almost an accident but I didn't remove it either, I looked at it as if it were something disconnected from me, with its own impulses and acts, its own culpability, and though it wasn't groping him or moving at all it *was* culpable, it was a violation, I knew this even as I looked at it in a kind of shock. I glanced at Z.'s face and saw he was looking too, not with any response I could read, and then he looked up, not at me or at the stage but straight ahead, his face clouded with an expression not of anger or dismay but of bewilderment, I thought, and coming to myself suddenly I snatched away my hand. I looked over at N., who seemed not to have noticed anything, he was still dancing, watching the show, absorbed in the music or in Andrea. Z. stood motionless beside me, his arm around my shoulder, his face not clouded anymore but blank. I looked away from him back to the stage, feeling a heat in my gut that I recognized as shame, but it wasn't sharp yet, it was distant or dulled, and though I knew in the next days I would be miserable with it I turned away from it now. Tomorrow you will feel it, I said to myself, feel it then, don't feel it now. I started dancing again, and when I moved Z. began to move too, he let his arm fall from my shoulder but began shifting side to side with the music, and soon he was smiling again. Maybe he thinks it was an accident, I thought, maybe it *was* an accident, maybe there's no need for shame, even though I knew that wasn't the case, or maybe he was so drunk he would forget it and then the only shame would be a private shame, the shame I was accustomed to, the shame that felt like home.

Z. stumbled again, this time falling toward N., who caught him and kept him on his feet. N. looked at me and laughed as Z. stood up again, closing his eyes and swaying; both of us put our hands on his shoulders to keep him upright. I looked at N. and tilted my head toward the entrance. We should go, I shouted, and he weaved his head from left to right. We each took one of Z.'s arms. We had to walk sideways and single file to make it through the crowd, though people tried to make room for us, smiling and moving out of our way as best they could. We must have been a familiar sight, two friends helping a third, and again I had the feeling of belonging with them, which was warm and present and drowned out my premonition of shame. We climbed the stairs and pushed out into the night, nodding at the two bouncers who didn't acknowledge us, and I sucked in great breaths as if I had been starving for air. Z. stumbled again, leaning hard against me, and we sat on the stairs to wait for the cab N. had called. Z. bent forward, his elbows propped on his knees, and moaned, and N. and I laughed at him. *Mnogo si slab, be*, I said, you're very weak, I expected better, and I gripped his shoulder to pull him to me. But then he slipped or lost his balance and fell across my lap, and a single fluent stream of vomit struck the pavement beside my shoes. He stayed in that position, draped across my lap, and I bent over him, as if to shield him from something, and rubbed his back, the fabric of his shirt damp with sweat. *Ne se chuvstvam dobre*, he said, pushing himself upright, I don't feel well, and N. told him not to worry, they were going home, he would sleep it off. They would go to Z.'s apartment, which was somewhere nearby, the studio his family kept and that Z. had claimed as his own, a place to take girls and have small gatherings, it was only big enough for five or six people, he had told me. He was still slumped against me,

I could feel his heat against my side. When the cab came we stood, N. and I pulling Z. up and leading him to the car. Will you be okay, I asked as Z. pulled his legs in, half lying across N.'s lap. But you're coming, N. said, don't you want to come with us, we can hang out at Z.'s place, and Z. echoed him, saying Yes, come, *Gospodine*, his voice slurred with drink. I stood with my hand on the car, hesitating, wanting to join them and imagining what might still happen, the possibilities of privacy with Z., I was tempted to try them. But I stepped back instead. No, I said, I have to go home, it's too late already. But thank you for tonight, I said, I had so much fun, thank you. It was a great night, Z. said, letting his head fall as I swung the door shut.

I didn't have to wait long for another taxi to appear, one pulled up almost right away, letting a couple out in front of the club. On the ride to Mladost I felt myself sinking into drunkenness, or felt drunkenness rise around me; even as I responded to the driver's small talk I closed my eyes and could feel my head roll to the side before I yanked it up again. I waved to the guards in their booth at the American College as the cab pulled away, and then I was beyond the glare of the floodlamps, on the dark road that led to the school. For years I had walked this path every day, morning and afternoon, with the weight of the day before me or with the relief of casting it off, and even now that I lived on campus I walked it often, to the store or the gym, to cabs waiting at the gates. I walked slowly now, feeling how easily I could stumble, taking a step or two to one side before I brought myself back to line. So this is what that is, I thought, remembering the drunks I had seen weaving in this way, imagining what I must look like to the guards in their booth, how maybe they had turned to watch me, people often watch drunks stumbling around, it amuses them, I don't know why. In me it has often aroused a darker feeling, pity or sometimes disdain; it wasn't funny at all, I would think, there was nothing innocent in it, it was a kind of willful abnegation of judgment, of responsibility. What have I done, I thought suddenly, what have I done. I turned onto the path between buildings, on the right the asphalt of the basketball court, where boys played soccer in the mornings, and on the left the row of academic buildings, in the most stately of which I had taught all my students, classes coming and going, Z. and N. coming twice, still boys in tenth grade and, two years later, something closer to men. It's a kind of performance, of course, all teaching is pretending; I had stood before them as a kind of poem of myself, an ideal image, when for a few hours every day I had been able to hide or mostly hide the disorder of my life, and if I hadn't succeeded entirely with Z. I had mostly succeeded, if he had seen glimpses of what I was he had never until tonight seen me fully. I had leered at him, I had touched him, I had been a caricature of myself, I thought, but that isn't true; I had been myself without impediment, maybe that's the way to say it.

I followed the path through the wooded part of campus, the trees that separate the main buildings from the faculty houses. The two floors of my cottage had been divided into apartments, of which mine was the loveliest, I thought, on the ground floor with windows facing into the trees. I had moved in less than a year before, tired of taking the bus each morning from my apartment off campus. I hadn't known how soon I would be leaving, not just Sofia but teaching

altogether, it had become unbearable, the drudgery and routine of it, earlier that spring I had realized I couldn't face
another year. A short set of stairs led to my door, four or
five steps, and as I began to climb them I stumbled, catching
myself with my hands and then falling onto my side against
the concrete, where I lay or half lay for a moment before sitting upright on the bottom step. I swallowed hard against a
wave of nausea, of nausea and something else, they were indistinguishable, seven years, I thought, seven years undone,
a betrayal of vocation. But I rejected this even as I thought
it, it wasn't my vocation, it was just something I had done, a
way I had passed the time; don't be so pious, something said
in me, and something else cringed away. I swallowed again,
I couldn't be sick here, everyone would see it, if I was going
to be sick I had to get inside. But though I willed myself to
stand I remained where I was, barely upright, my hands but-
tressed at my sides and my torso leaning forward, swaying a
little. I was exaggerating or making excuses, it wasn't so bad
or it was worse. You can't know tonight, I thought, in the
morning you'll know, and I feared what I would feel, how
my actions would look in the light of day, those were the
words I used, the light of day, I was thinking in old phrases.

I tried to stand again, lifting myself a few inches before I
dropped back down. I heard a sound then and looked up, and
saw coming up the path toward me the fat shape of Mama
Dog, her tail beating in the dark. She was the only dog allowed on campus; for years she had kept other dogs away,
but now she was too old to guard anything, and she spent
most of the day sleeping, on the porches of our houses or

beside the guards where they sat in the shade. She was always happy to see me, I gave her treats sometimes, but I didn't have anything for her now, and I told her this, *Nyamam nishto*, opening my empty hands. She cocked her head, that look of understanding dogs give, or of wanting to understand, their demand for attention. *Obicham te*, I said to her, I love you, but tonight I don't have anything, go away, I said, *mahai se*, and I made a shooing motion with my hand. But she didn't go, she stood staring at me, the movement of her tail slowing just slightly, and then she inched forward and pressed her snout against my hand, her nose wet in my palm. Still I didn't respond, but she insisted, jerking her nose up as if to toss my hand to her head, where she wanted to be scratched. I laughed and said Okay, Mama, okay, as I raked my fingers through her fur. She whined happily and came closer, pressing her trunk against my leg and rippling her body in that puppyish movement that communicates joy better than anything we can manage, and I used both hands to scratch along her sides, feeling bits of leaf and pine needles and accumulated grime. You're filthy, I said, but I love you, and I bent my face down to hers, touching our foreheads together and gripping her in something like a hug. She tolerated this briefly, and then she tilted her snout slightly up and quickly licked my face, her tongue wet across my lips. I pulled back, making a sound of disgust and wiping my lips clean, but then I laughed again.

She pressed against me more insistently, rubbing the top of her head against my jeans. She wanted a treat, and wanted more to be let inside. She had been a house dog once, I had heard, years ago she had belonged to a foreign teacher who left her behind when he went back to the States, she loved to sleep in our houses. But we had been told it wasn't allowed; she was almost always dirty, and though she was treated for fleas and ticks you could never be sure, she was an outdoor dog now, we shouldn't encourage her. But there was no one around to admonish me, and so *Ela*, I said to her, come on, and then I stood, successfully this time, maybe because Mama kept her side pressed against me, as if to prop me up as I kept one hand braced against the brick wall of the house. She whined at the door as I fumbled the key into the lock. Okay, Mama, I said soothingly again, okay. I would take the box of treats from the cabinet above the sink, I would put towels down on the kitchen floor so she would have a soft place to lie down. She was dirty but what was a little dirt, I thought as I turned the latch, I should have let you in a long time ago, I said, I'm sorry. I pushed the door open and she went ahead of me into the house, going just a few feet before she dropped onto the tile of the entranceway, a spot she claimed as if it had long been hers, and gave a quick deep sigh as she laid her head on her paws. She kept her eyes on me as I tossed my keys in the little dish by the door, her tail more subdued but still striking the wall beside her as I put my bag down, waiting for the dizziness to pass. Okay, Mama, I said again, you sleep there, we'll sleep and in the morning we'll feel better, though I feared I wouldn't feel better, in body and spirit both I thought I would likely feel much worse. And then, because the dizziness didn't pass or maybe because I wanted her warmth next to me, I lowered myself to the floor, I stretched myself out beside her and laid one hand on her flank. We'll sleep, I said again, and she rolled onto her side, her stomach toward me, and placed one of her paws against my chest. It would leave a mark, I knew, I would have to scrub it out in the morning, but what did it matter, I thought as I closed my eyes, what does it matter, why not let it stay.

ACKNOWLEDGMENTS

Excerpts from this book first appeared, often in very different versions, in *The Iowa Review*, *The New Yorker*, *The Paris Review*, *A Public Space*, *The Sewanee Review*, and *StoryQuarterly*. Special thanks to Brigid Hughes, Cressida Leyshon, Adam Ross, Nicole Rudick, and Lorin Stein.

A residency fellowship from the Lannan Foundation made it possible for me to complete this book. Thanks also to the Next Page Foundation and the Elizabeth Kostova Foundation for residencies in Bulgaria.

Many thanks to Anna Stein, Claire Nozieres, Morgan Oppenheimer, and Lucy Luck for the care they've taken with this book.

Thank you to Mitzi Angel for her brilliant, collaborative editing, and to everyone at FSG and Picador (U.S. and U.K.), especially Eric Chinski, Kris Doyle, Anna deVries, and Brian Gittis. Special and endless thanks to Camilla Elworthy.

For reading early versions of this book, in whole or in part, thank you to Jamel Brinkley, Kevin Brockmeier, Lan Samantha Chang, Ilya Kaminsky, Dimiter Kenarov, D. Wystan Owen, and Alan Pierson.

For all things, thank you to Luis Muñoz.